island stories

'The lyrical beauty and vivid atmosphere of Aran are exemplified in the fiction and true life stories by such world-renowned writers as Synge, O'Flaherty, Sean and Maurice O'Sullivan. In this carefully selected anthology of extracts, including many stories by seanchái, the reader comes to appreciate the true island mind.'

NEWSLETTER, BELFAST

'. . . a luxury of texture astonishing in comparison to the bleakness of the landscape that fired such imaginations.'

WESTERN JOURNAL

First published 1977 by O'Brien Educational Ltd., 20 Victoria Road, Dublin 6.

Reprinted 1980, 1982, 1984 and 1986.

ISBN 0-86278-117-5

10 9 8 7 6 5

The Curriculum Development Unit was established in 1972. It is funded by the City of Dublin Vocational Education Committee. It is managed jointly by the City of Dublin Vocational Education Committee, Trinity College, Dublin, and the Department of Education. This book forms part of the Humanities Curriculum.

Director: *Anton Trant*
Deputy Director: *Tony Crooks*
Humanities Team:
Tony Crooks, Co-ordinator 1972-79
Nora Godwin, 1973-79, Co-ordinator 1979-
Agnes McMahon, 1975-76
Bernard O'Flaherty, 1976-78
Dermot Stokes, 1977-82
Ann Treacy, 1978-80

This collection has been researched and edited by Paul O'Sullivan with revisions by Nora Godwin.

Printed by Brough, Cox & Dunn Ltd.

Prior to publication, the following schools were involved in the development, use and revision of the collection. The suggestions and comments of the teachers in these schools have been used as a basis for the edition.

Colaiste Dhulaigh, Coolock; Colaiste Eanna, Cabra; Colaiste Eoin, Finglas; Coolmine Community School, Clonsilla; Gonzaga College, Dublin; Liberties Vocational School, Dublin; Scoil Ide, Finglas; Vocational School, Ballyfermot; Vocational School for Boys, Clogher Road; Vocational School, Crumlin Road.

contents

a day's hunting

maurice o'sullivan

Maurice O'Sullivan was reared on the Blasket Islands off the coast of Co. Kerry. *Fiche Blian ag Fás,* his account of his boyhood on the islands during the period 1910-1920, was translated into English as *Twenty Years A-Growing.* This excerpt describes an expedition by the young Maurice and his friend Tomás, to capture sea birds on the cliffs at the Great Blasket.

THE NEXT DAY, A SUNDAY, was very fine, the sea calm, and not a sound to be heard but the murmur of the waves breaking on the White Strand and the footsteps of men walking down to the quay on their way out to the mainland to Mass.

There were six or seven curraghs out in Mid-Bay by this time, the men in them stripped to their shirts. Soon I saw Tomás coming down.

'God be with you, Tomás.'

'The same God with you. Wouldn't it be a fine day on the hill? Would you have any courage for it?'

'Your soul to the devil, let us go,' said I.

We went up the hill-road together, sweet music in our ears from the heather-hens on the summit. Each of us had a dog.

'Maybe,' said Tomás, 'we would get a dozen of puffins back in the Fern Bottom and another dozen of rabbits. I have a great dog for them.'

We reached Horses' Pound, the heat of the sun cracking the stones and a head of sweat on us. We sat down on a tuft of grass. The devil if Tomás had not a pipe and tobacco. He lit it and handed it to me. 'I don't smoke,' said I. 'Try it,' said he.

When I had had my fill of it, I gave it back to him and stretched myself out on my back in the heat of the sun. But, if so, I soon began to feel Horses' Pound going round me. I was frightened. Tomás was singing to himself.

'Tomás,' said I at last, 'something is coming over me.'

He looked at me. 'It is too much of the pipe you have had. Throw up, and nothing will be on you.'

I would rather have been dead than the way I was, wheezing and whinnying ever and ever till at last I threw up.

When we got to our feet we could not find the dogs. We whistled but they did not come.

'Beauty, Beauty, Beauty,' I cried aloud, for that was the name of my dog.

'Topsy, Topsy, Topsy,' cried Tomás.

At that moment my dog appeared with a rabbit across her mouth. 'My heart for ever, Beauty!' I cried. Then Topsy returned with her mouth empty. 'You can see now which is the better dog,' said I.

We went on to the Fern Bottom and soon my dog had scented a puffin. We began digging the hole but the ground was too firm and we had to give it up. Off with us then as far as White Rocks.

'We have a good chance now for a dozen of rabbits, for the burrows are very shallow here.'

'Look,' said I, 'Beauty has scented something.'

Down we ran. I thrust my hand into the burrow and drew out a fine fat rabbit.

'Your soul to the devil, Topsy has scented another,' shouted Tomás, and away with him down to the hole. Before long we had a dozen and a half.

'We had better take a rest now,' said Tomás, sitting down on the grass. He took out the pipe again and offered it to me. 'Musha, keep it away,' said I; 'I have bought sense from it already.'

It was midday now, the sun in the height of its power and a great heat in it. While we were talking, Tomás rose up on his elbow: 'Do you know where we will go for the rest of the day?'

'Where?'

'Gathering sea-gulls' eggs in the Scórnach.'

Away we went till we reached its mouth. Looking down at the cliff, a feeling of dizziness came over me.

'What mother's son could go down there, Tomás?'

'Arra, man,' said he, with a laugh, 'you only lack practice. I was the same way myself when I came here the first day with Shaun O'Shea. He was for ever urging me till I agreed to go down with him.'

'Maybe you are right. We had better hide the rabbits here on top and not be carrying them down and up again.'

We began to search for a suitable hole.

'There is a good one here, Tomás.'

'The devil, the gulls would find them out there.'

At last we found a place and we did not leave as much as a pinhole without covering it with fern and sods of earth. Then we turned our faces towards the cliff.

Tomás was down before me leaping as light as a goat through the screes, and no wonder, for it is amongst them he had spent his life. 'Take it fine and easy,' he said to me, 'for fear your foot would loosen a stone and hit me on the head as it went down the hill. It is then you would be raising a clamour, Maurice, when you would see me falling over the cliff.'

'Don't be talking that way, Tomás. You make me shiver.'

A cold sweat was coming out on me with the eeriness of the place. I stopped and looked up. When I saw the black rugged cliff standing straight above I began to tremble still more. I looked down and there was nothing below me but the blue depth of the sea: 'God of Virtues!' I cried, 'isn't it a dangerous place I am in!'

I could see Tomás still climbing down like a goat, without a trouble or care in the world. There was a great din in the gully, shining white with the droppings of the sea-birds – kittiwakes, herring-gulls, puffins, guillemots, sea-ravens, razor-bills, black-backed gulls and petrels – each with its own cry and its own nest built in the rock.

I was looking at them and watching them until before long the dizziness left me, while I thought what a hard life they had, foraging for food like any sinner.

As I was thinking, I saw a puffin making straight towards me in from the sea. It was quite near me now, and I saw it had a bundle of sprats across its mouth. It came nearer and nearer until it was only five yards away. It was likely going to land on the rock, I thought, so I lay down in the long heather which was growing around. It came in fearlessly and I made a grab at it with my hand. But it had gone into a burrow beside me. The entrance was covered with bird dung. I began digging it out and it was easy enough, for I had only to thrust my hand back and lift up the ledge of a stone. There was a fine fat whippeen in it. I thrust my hand in to draw it out, but, if so, I wished I had not, for it gave me a savage bite with its beak. When I caught it by the throat it dug its claws into me so that my hand was streaming with blood At last I drew it out and killed it.

I arose and looked down. Tomás was nowhere to be seen.

'Tomás,' I cried.

'Tomás,' said the echo, answering me.

'Well,' came up from Tomás far below.

'Well,' repeated the echo, the way you would swear by the Book there were four of us on the cliff. It seemed to me he was miles below me. God of Virtues, said I to myself, he will fall over the cliff as sure as I live. I will go no farther myself anyway.

I was wandering to and fro among the screes until I came across another burrow with dung at its mouth. Faith, I have another, said I, taking courage. I began to dig. Soon I had drawn out a fine fat puffin. At the end of my wanderings I had three dozen.

I was now the happiest hunter on the hills of Kerry. I sat down on a stone and drew out the bundle of bread I had brought with me for the day. I ate it hungrily. When I got up and looked at the whippeens I had thrown in a heap in the hollow beside me, I wondered how I would carry them home. Then I remembered I had a rope round my waist. I untied it, took hold of a dozen of the birds, put their heads together and tied up the dozen in a single knot. I did the same with the second dozen and the third, till I had them all on the rope.

The sun was now as round as a plate beyond the Tearacht to the west, and a path of glittering golden light stretching as far as the horizon over the sea. I looked down, but Tomás was not coming yet, for he was a man who never showed haste or hurry so long as plunder was to be had. I gave a whistle. The echo answered me as before. Soon after I heard him shouting, 'I am coming!'

Hundreds of birds were flying around, rabbits leaping from one clump of thrift to another, a fragrant smell from the white heather and the fern, big vessels far out on the horizon you would think were on fire in the sunlight, a heat haze here and there in the ravines, and Kerry diamonds lying all around weakening my eyes with their sparkle.

Now I could see Tomás climbing slowly up, his face dirty and smeared with earth and no jersey on him. I laughed aloud when I saw the look of him. He was climbing from ledge to ledge till he was within a few yards of me. He had taken off his jersey, tied a cord round the neck of it and thrown it over his back with whatever booty he had inside it. Coming up to me he put down the jersey carefully on the ground.

'The devil take you, Tomás, what have you got?'

'I have guillemots' eggs, razor-bills' eggs and sea-gulls eggs, my boy,' said he, wiping the sweat from his forehead with his cap.

'Your soul to the devil, why didn't you come down, man, and we would have had twice as many?'

'I was too frightened,' said I, pretending I had got no plunder myself. 'I dare say it is as well for us to be starting now.' And going across to my bundle I threw it over my back.

'What have you there?'

'Puffins in plenty.'

'Where did you get them?'

'Here in the scree without stirring out of it.'

'By God, you are the best hunter I ever met.'

We were moving on now up to the head of the cliff. We went on from ledge to ledge and from clump to clump. When we were up at last we lay down to rest.

'Wait till you see the eggs I have,' said Tomás, opening his jersey.

They were a lovely sight, covered with black and red spots. 'We have had a great hunt,' said I.

'Very good indeed. Have you many whippeens?'

'Three dozen.'

'Och, we will never carry them all home. But it is where the trouble will be now if the eggs are not clean after all our pains.'

'Can't you see for yourself they are clean?' said I, laughing.

'Ah, that is not the cleanness I mean; but come with me and we will soon know.'

We went down to the south to a big pool of water in a bog-hole. 'Look now,' said he, taking up an egg, 'if this egg is hatching it will float on the water, but if it is clean it will sink.'

He threw in the egg. It remained floating.

'Och, the devil take it, there is a chick in that one.'

He took it out and broke it against a stone and sure enough there was a chick in it. 'Faith,' said he, 'it is a good beginning.' He put in another in the water and it was the same way again. 'The devil a clean one among them,' said I. 'I am afraid you are right,' said he, throwing in another and not one of them sinking.

He lost heart then after all his walking in the run of the day and all for nothing. Seeing how despondent he was on account of it: 'Don't mind,' said I; 'haven't we enough, each of us with a dozen and a half of rabbits and a dozen and a half of whippeens?'

We divided the spoils, and when we had all done up in bundles we were ready for the journey home. I looked at Tomás again and laughed.

'I don't know in the world why you are laughing at me since morning.'

'Because anyone would think you were an ape you are so dirty.'

'Faith, if I am as dirty as you are, the yellow devil is on me.'

'What would you say to giving ourselves a good dip in the pool?'

'It is a good idea.'

We stripped off all we had and went in, and when we were dressed again we felt so fresh we could have walked the hill twice over.

'The devil, that was a grand dip.'

'Arra, man, I am not the same after it. Now in the name of God let us turn our faces homewards.'

It was growing late. The sun was sinking on the horizon, the dew falling heavily as the air cooled, the dock-leaves closing up for the night, sea-birds crying as they came back to their young, rabbits rushing through the fern as they left their warrens, the sparkle gone out of the Kerry diamonds and a lonesome look coming over the ravines.

'It is night, Tomás.'

'It is. Isn't there a great stretch on the day?'

'There is, and my people will likely be anxious about me for they don't know where I am. They will say it is into some hole I have fallen.'

'Ah, mo léir, it is often I was out and it is only midnight would bring me home.'

'But I am not the same as you.'

'Why not? Amn't I human the same as yourself?'

'Ah, you are an old dog on the hill and your people are used to your being out late and early. It is the first time for me.'

We were now in sight of the village, lamps lit in every house, dogs barking, the houses and rocks clearly reflected in the sea which lay below them without a stir like a well of fresh water, the moon climbing up behind Cnoc a-choma, big and round and as yellow as gold.

We said good-bye and parted, Tomás to his house and I to mine.

mackerel nets

thomas o'flaherty

Thomas O'Flaherty was a native of Inishmore who spent his childhood and part of his adult life on the island. His book *Cliffmen of the West* describes the daily life of the island as he experienced it in the period. "Mackerel Nets", an excerpt from this book, tells of a narrow escape which O'Flaherty had, along with his uncle and two of his cousins, while hauling nets into their curragh.

"IF THE NETS ARE NOT TAKEN when the current is slack with the changing of the tide, they'll never be taken," my uncle said. My father nodded his head towards his crew. My uncle beckoned to me and to my two cousins – sons of an uncle who had died – to come.

I, being the tallest of the four, crawled under the curach, got my shoulders under the first stand. Two men, one on each side of the prow, lifted the boat with me. When I was straight, holding up the prow, another man got under the rear seat and straightened up. A third shouldered a middle seat, and then this boat, that has been likened when carried in this fashion to a "gigantic beetle on stilts", was walked to the water. A fourth member of the crew followed with the oars on his shoulder. Our curach was the first to be laid on the strand ready for launching. We turned her prow to the surf and put the eight oars on the pins. Several men who had not yet decided to go to sea gathered around our curach. We pushed her out until she was afloat. Then the four of us took our seats. We held our oars poised over the water, ready to start rowing at a signal from the look-out man. Six men held the curach straight in the face of the waves while we waited for a lull. Then the look-out shouted hoarsely: "Stick her out! Give her the oars!"

The six men dug their pampootie-clad feet into the sand and pushed the curach quickly towards the sea. Our eight oars struck the water simultaneously. We seemed to be rowing in a pond for a moment, the sea was so smooth. Then the curach rose sharply and almost stood on end, straight as an arrow in a big sea. Down she came on the other side with a crash that set the teeth shaking in our mouths.

As the first sea fell on the strand we rose on another, not as dangerous as the first because we were in deeper water, but bad enough to prove our undoing if the curach's head was turned an inch too far to the right or left.

We rowed, putting our oars far forward and bringing them to a feather with a graceful flourish. My uncle sang joyously in a voice that was everything but melodious. We were now out of danger, in the long lazy swell of the deep water.

As we rowed towards our nets, we could see the prow of another curach rising over the crest of a sea, then disappearing in the trough. Then another curach got safely through the gauntlet of shore breakers.

"The first one is my brother's curach," my uncle said, with a touch of pride. "The one after him is Mícheal Mór O'Dioráin's."

The three most daring skippers leaving Port Murvey were now on the sea, and soon most of the curachs would be out.

We took our markings and shortly we were right over the first pocán. It was attached to the tail end of two pieces of net. Here the water was deep and we had no trouble taking them. The next two pieces were also brought in safely. Now, we must go right up to the edge of the Big Breaker.

"It should be on the point of full tide," my uncle said. "Unless we have them in before the tide turns, we'll have to use the knife on them. This place will be in foam in a few minutes."

We pulled right up to the pocán. One of my cousins took in the buoy, untied it and tossed it to me. I handed it to my uncle, who placed it in the bow with the other two.

Then my cousin stood on the transom and started to haul in the nets. He had a long sharp knife between his teeth. My uncle and I were on our oars. The four oars were on the pins, stretched along the side of the curach, the blades inside. A third man was stowing the nets.

The Big Breaker was between us and Conamara. My uncle kept his steely blue eyes on the giant ridge of water. We had one net aboard and about half the second when he noticed what looked like a puff of smoke on the crest of the breaker.

"Give them the knife!" my uncle shouted to the man on the transom. "Cut, cut, cut! Lay the sticks on her! Every man on the oars!"

Quick as a flash the long, sharp knife fell on the cork rope, severing it in two. The meshes tore with a ripping noise as the curach darted ahead impelled by the sudden, simultaneous stroke of six oars. The foot-rope appeared for a moment on the transom and in the next was severed with one dexterous slash. The knife-man leaped to his seat and now eight oars were bending in a race with the mighty comber that bore down on our stern. It was a race against death.

We turned the curach's head straight towards the strand, the shortest cut in the direction of deep water. The Big Breaker was getting ready to crash all over the shallows. The one following was a forerunner of others, even more dangerous. At the shallowest spot the mighty reef was already white, the moving crest leaving a cloud of spray in its wake.

We strained at the oars, my uncle urging us on. Usually harsh, he was now encouraging us with endearing expressions. We put all our strength into the pull, in such a way that every muscle in the body was in action. We got the last ounce of motion out of every stroke.

"Another minute" – my uncle began. He did not finish the sentence, for at that moment as if by magic the mighty wave suddenly towered at our stern and seemed to be looking down on us, the slightest suggestion of foam on its crest.

"Dead on the oars!" my uncle hissed. "Hold her steady!" Eight oars were dug into the sea as we kept our eyes straight ahead and held the curach's stern straight in the breaker. Would it break on top of us? We did not even look at one another, let alone speak. We sat like stone idols on the thwarts as if we had become suddenly petrified. We were dumb with horror of the monster wave into whose maw we might be sucked any moment.

Suddenly the transom rose until the curach almost stood straight on her prow. Quickly, but in what seemed an eternity to us, the sea swept by, breaking a few yards ahead. For the moment we were safe, unless another one came right after the first. No! We were safe. We bent to our oars again and soon we were in deep water.

We had five of our six nets. The sixth and one anchor would

be lost. Not so bad at all!

By this time the sea was bursting on every shallow in the bay. We lighted our pipes and rowed proudly and contentedly towards the shore.

"We stopped just in time," said the knife-man. "Another moment – "

"If your knife hadn't got the footrope the first slash, 'tis talking to Peter by now we'd be," said my uncle.

the kelp burners

thomas o'flaherty

In this passage from *Cliffmen of the West,* Thomas O'Flaherty describes a night spent, as a boy, helping the neighbouring men at the kelp kiln.

THEN THERE AROSE INTO THE atmosphere between me and Conamara billows of light smoke floating lazily and vanishing. It was the smoke from a kelp kiln, burning on the White Shore. I longed to see a kelp kiln in action. But I was considered too young to be out at night, and sure there was no fun watching a kelp kiln burning in the daytime! I would ask my mother's permission. She couldn't refuse me anything.

Presently my mother came home with a large can of milk. She noticed my gloomy look and asked me what was the trouble. I did not answer for a while. Then I told her I would like to go to the White Shore where men from Oatquarter were burning kelp. She was silent for a moment.

"They'll be drinking poitín, *a stóir,*" she said. "And I don't want you to be around where that cursed stuff is."

"But I have the pledge, mother," I answered.

"That's true, O little son," she said. "Your father would be angry with you, I'm afraid."

"He wouldn't if you gave me leave to go," I urged. She smiled and then she wept and she took me in her arms and kissed me, and for a moment I lost all desire to see the kelp fire – I was so happy. But soon the thirst for adventure overwhelmed me and I looked appealingly at her.

"The teacher wants me to write an essay about kelp-making," I said.

"Put down the kettle and we'll make a cup of tea," she said. "But you mustn't stay late."

It was nearing sunset when I started towards the White Shore. Birds whistled in the ivy clumps on the rocks and in the sally gardens. Cows lowed. Now and then a sheep bleated. Voices of men echoed from the hollow places in the cliffs. I walked jauntily along whistling for myself. For the first time in my life I would be away from home for the night without a guardian. I was getting to be a man!

I was happy to the point of ecstasy. I pictured myself sitting down on a cock of dry seaweed or on a boulder watching the darting flames and the waves of thick black smoke that became lighter as they ascended to the heavens. Perhaps I would have the privilege of helping to carry the weed to the kiln. I would be given tea and bread and treated like a grown-up man. Perhaps I would be praised and that somebody would say: *"Ní ó'n ngréin ná ó'n ngaoith a thógais é* – It is not from the sun or the wind you took it, O son of Michael!"

I had a mile and a half of a walk in front of me.

Every year about the first of May the Big Breaker half way between Aran and Conamara rears its crest and sends mighty waves speeding towards the shore. All along the bayside of the island lesser breakers come in its wake, and the red seaweed that grows on the shallow places is torn up by the roots and carried to land by the currents. The best kelp is made from this red weed if it gets to the shore quickly, and is spread out to dry before it loses some of the precious juice in deep sea holes and in the burrows under the rocks. Seaweed that is washed ashore on a sandy beach is almost useless for kelpmaking.

To the shores of boulders and pebbles the men take their straddled horses, a basket on each side with ropes made of horse-hair attached. High over the straddle they pile the seaweed and hold it together with the ropes. And those hard Aran ponies of the Conamara strain pick their way over slippery, moss-covered flags, between large boulders and pebbles that give way under pressure of hoof, with the sureness of goats among the crags of a mountain.

As I stepped along I thought of the work involved in making kelp from the time the first wisp was gathered until the burned seaweed was in the hands of the buyer. Whatever money was made out of kelp was certainly paid for with hard labour.

When the islanders gathered seaweed in the winter and spring to manure their potato gardens they saved the long rods on which the red seaweed grew, laid them on the limestone fences to dry, and then put them in cocks. These rods are rich in iodine.

No seaweed was saved for kelp until the potato gardens were manured. The seaweed that was washed ashore this time of the year was not as good quality as what came in at the end of spring and in the early summer. Furthermore it rained almost continuously during those seasons, making it almost impossible to dry the seaweed. And the potato was the mainstay of the island. As the people would say: *"Cothuíonn sé duine 'gus beithíoch* – It nourishes man and beast."

The seaweed is spread along the roadside or in fields near by the shore. When it is thoroughly dried it is put in cocks until burning time.

When there is a spring tide a long ribbony weed of deep-red colour is cut at low water. It is rated next to red weed in iodine content. Sometimes this seaweed is brought up from the bottom by means of long poles, called *croísiní* because of the wooden blade at the end of the pole which gives it the appearance of a cross. Black weed is also used for kelp-making, but is considered much inferior to the red seaweeds.

The sun was setting in the north-west when I reached the White Shore. It was Michael Donal who was burning, or to give him his full birthday title Michael son of Donal, son of Patrick son of Michael, son of Bartholomew. He was a kinsman of mine so I made bold to ask him if I could help. He smiled and said that he needed a strong man that very minute.

"Do you see that big cock over there" he said. "Well, get a ladder, climb up on it and start tearing the dry fern off the top of it. Don't hurt yourself, son!"

It was an old cock of seaweed that was there since the previous autumn, and it was thatched with fern and heather to protect it from the rain.

Up I went on the cock and I began to tear off the thatch. I broke the straw ropes or *súgáin* with which it was tied. Every now and then I stopped to watch the blazing kiln and the men feeding the devouring fire.

The kiln was young and the men were going light with the seaweed. The coffin-like incinerator was twenty feet long, three feet wide and one and a half feet high. A fire was started with turf, sticks and dry fern. Once the seaweed got to burn with a little breeze, a deluge would not drown it.

I was not long working when Michael's two daughters came with bread and tea. Michael called me.

"Come down here, son, and have the full of your mouth," he said in Gaelic, the modest way an Aran Islander has of inviting you to gorge yourself with food.

Seven of us sat on the shore to eat. The bread was buttered while hot. This was a feast for a bishop. There was enough bread and tea to feed twice the number. Anybody who came around while the meal was being eaten was forced to share in the food. Two men were taking care of the kiln. With a fresh breeze, sprung up out of the northwest, it was burning evenly from end to end.

It was pitch dark now a short distance from the kiln. Like ghosts the two men who were feeding the flames would appear out of the gloom with armfuls of seaweed and vanish again. The two girls who brought the meal sat on boulders in the glare of the light and looked intently at the fire. The men paid no attention to the them, though they were goodlooking girls. Perhaps they were afraid of irascible old Michael. I looked at them and wondered what they were thinking about. Perhaps they were thinking that part of the price of the kelp would pay their way to America. That was the constant thought in those days. As for me, my ambition at that moment was to grow up in Aran, fish, plant potatoes and make kelp. I was in my glory thinking I was doing a man's share of the work.

I listened eagerly to the conversation of the men. They talked of olden times and of the great kilns of kelp they burned, of going to Kilkerrin on the mainland to sell it and the adventures they had. That was the way with Aran Islanders. They had appropriate stories for every season of the year. In the mackerel season they told stories of great hauls of mackerel and the dangers they encountered taking the nets, the prices they got for the fish and their fights with the buyers. It was the same way when they were engaged manuring, planting or digging potatoes, killing rock birds in the high cliffs on the south side of the island, thatching the houses or going down the cliffs for wrack.

About two o'clock the horizon on the north-east lightened and soon crimsoned. The sun was coming up and I was getting sleepy and felt like lying down. Michael advised me to go home and to bed. I told him I would after I saw them rake the kiln. Michael nodded.

"Go light on her now " he ordered. "It's time we gave her the first raking."

Then the men got hold of long iron rods and stripping to the waist they raked the burnt seaweed in the kiln from end to end and from side to side. They shouted to each other to work harder as the sweat poured from their bodies. When the kelp began to run in a molten mass they stopped and threw more seaweed on the kiln.

The kiln would be burned about twelve o'clock the next night. I would be there if I got my mother's consent. I made for home at a steady trot. When I got to the door I lifted the latch noiselessly hoping nobody would hear me come in. But the dog barked a greeting. I sneaked to bed but I was barely inside the clothes when my mother came, put her hand on my forehead and kissed me. Neither of us spoke. I was soon asleep.

Spring Sowing

Liam O'Flaherty

IT WAS STILL DARK WHEN MARTIN DELANEY and his wife Mary got up. Martin stood in his shirt by the window a long time looking out, rubbing his eyes and yawning, while Mary raked out the fire coals that had lain hidden in the ashes on the hearth all night. Outside, cocks were crowing and a white streak was rising from the ground, as it were, and beginning to scatter the darkness. It was a February morning, dry, cold and starry.

The couple sat down to their breakfast of tea, bread and butter, in silence. They had only been married the previous autumn and it was hateful leaving a warm bed at such an early hour. They both felt in a bad humour and ate, wrapped in their thoughts. Martin with his brown hair and eyes, his freckled face and his little fair moustache, looked too young to be married, and his wife looked hardly more than a girl, red-cheeked and blue-eyed, her black hair piled at the rear of her head with a large comb gleaming in the middle of the pile, Spanish fashion. They were both dressed in rough homespuns, and both wore the loose white frieze shirt that Inverara peasants use for work in the fields.

They ate in silence, sleepy and bad humoured and yet on fire with excitement, for it was the first day of their first spring sowing as man and wife. And each felt the glamour of that day on which they were to open up the earth together and plant seeds in it. So they sat in silence and bad humour, for somehow the imminence of an event that had been long expected, loved, feared and prepared for, made them dejected. Mary, with her shrewd woman's mind, munched her bread and butter and thought of... Oh, what didn't she think of? Of as many things as there are in life does a woman think in the first joy and anxiety of her mating.

But Martin's mind was fixed on one thought. Would he be able to prove himself a man worthy of being the head of a family by doing his spring sowing well?

In the barn after breakfast, when they were getting the potato seeds and the line for measuring the ground and the spade, a cross word or two passed between them, and when Martin fell over a basket in the half-darkness of the barn, he swore and said that a man would be better off dead than... But before he could finish what he was going to say, Mary had her arms around his waist and her face to his. 'Martin,' she said, 'let us not begin this day cross with one another.' And there was a tremor in her voice. And somehow, as they embraced and Martin kept mumbling in his awkward peasant's voice, 'pulse of my heart, treasure of my life,' and such traditional phrases, all their irritation and sleepiness left them. And they stood there embracing until at last Martin pushed her from him with pretended roughness and said: 'Come, come, girl, it will be sunset before we begin at this rate.'

Still, as they walked silently in their rawhide shoes, through the little hamlet, there was not a soul about. Lights were glimmering in the windows of a few cabins. The sky had a big grey crack in it in the east, as if it were going to burst in order to give birth to the sun. Birds were singing somewhere at a distance. Martin and Mary rested their baskets of seeds on a fence outside the village and Martin whispered to Mary proudly: 'We are first, Mary.' And they both looked back at the little cluster of cabins, that was the centre of their world, with throbbing hearts. For the joy of spring had now taken complete hold of them.

They reached the little field where they were to sow. It was a little triangular patch of ground under an ivy-covered limestone hill. The little field had been manured with seaweed some weeks before, and the weeds had rotted and whitened on the grass. And there was a big red heap of fresh seaweed lying in a corner by the fence to be spread under the seeds as they were laid. Martin, in spite of the cold, threw off everything above his waist except his striped woollen shirt. Then he spat on his hands, seized his spade and cried: 'Now you are going to see what kind of a man you have, Mary.'

'There, now,' said Mary, tying a little shawl closer under her chin. 'Aren't we boastful this early hour of the morning? Maybe I'll wait till sunset to see what kind of a man I have got.'

The work began. Martin measured the ground by the southern fence for the first ridge, a strip of ground four feet wide, and he placed the line along the edge and pegged it at each end. Then he spread fresh seaweed over the strip. Mary filled her apron with seeds and began to lay them in rows, four, three, four. When she was a little distance down the ridge Martin advanced with spade to the head eager to commence.

'Now in the name of God,' he cried, spitting on his palms, 'let us raise the first sod! '

'Oh, Martin, wait till I'm with you!' cried Mary, dropping her seeds on the ridge and running up to him. Her fingers outside her woollen mittens were numb with the cold, and she couldn't wipe them in her apron. Her cheeks seemed to be on fire. She put an arm round Martin's waist and stood looking at the green sod his spade was going to cut, with the excitement of a little child.

'Now for God's sake, girl, keep back! ' said Martin gruffly. 'Suppose anybody saw us trapesing about like this in the field of our spring sowing, what would they take us for but a pair of useless, soft, empty-headed people that would be sure to die of the hunger. Huh! ' He spoke very rapidly, and his eyes were fixed on the ground before him. His eyes had a wild, eager light in them as if some primeval impulse were burning within his brain and driving out every other desire but that of asserting his manhood and of subjugating the earth.

'Oh, what do we care who is looking? ' said Mary; but she drew back at the same time and gazed distantly at the ground. Then Martin cut the sod, and pressing the spade deep into the earth with his foot, he turned up the first sod with a crunching sound as the grass roots were dragged out of the earth. Mary sighed and walked back hurriedly to her seeds with furrowed brows. She picked up her seeds and began to spread them rapidly to drive out the sudden terror that had seized her at that moment when the first sod was turned up and she saw the fierce, hard look in her husband's eyes, that were unconscious of her presence. She became suddenly afraid of that pitiless, cruel earth, the peasant's slave master, that would keep her chained to hard work and poverty all her life until she would sink again into its bosom. Her short-lived love was gone. Henceforth she was only her husband's helper to till the earth. And Martin, absolutely without thought, worked furiously, covering the ridge with black earth, his sharp spade gleaming white as he whirled it sideways to beat the sods.

Then as the sun rose the little valley beneath the ivy-covered hills became dotted with white frieze shirts, and everywhere men worked madly without speaking and women spread seeds. There was no heat in the light of the sun, and there was a sharpness in the still thin air that made the men jump on their spade shafts ferociously and beat the sods as if they were living enemies. Birds hopped silently before the spades, with their heads cocked sideways, watching for worms. Made brave by hunger they often dashed under the spades to secure their food.

Then when the sun reached a certain point all the women went back to the village to get dinner for their men, and the men worked on without stopping. Then the women returned, almost running, each carrying a tin can with a flannel tied around it and a little bundle tied with a white cloth. Martin threw down his spade when Mary arrived back in the field. Smiling at one another they sat under the hill for their meal. It was the same as their breakfast, tea and bread and butter.

'Ah,' said Martin, when he had taken a long draught of tea from his mug, 'is there anything in this world as fine as eating dinner out in the open like this after doing a good morning's work? There, I have done two ridges and a half. That's more than any man in the village could do. Ha! ' And he looked at his wife proudly.

'Yes, isn't it lovely,' said Mary, looking at the black ridges wistfully. She was just munching her bread and butter. The hurried trip to the village and the trouble of getting the tea ready had robbed her of her appetite. She had to keep blowing at the turf fire with the rim of her skirt, and the smoke nearly blinded her. But now, sitting on that grassy knoll, with the valley all round glistening with fresh seaweed and a light smoke rising from the freshly turned earth, a strange joy swept over her. It overpowered that other feeling of dread that had been with her during the morning.

Martin ate heartily, revelling in his great thirst and his great hunger, with every pore of his body open to the pure air. And he looked around at his neighbours' fields boastfully, comparing them with his own. Then he looked at his wife's little round black head and felt very proud of having her as his own. He leaned back on his elbow and took her hand in his. Shyly and in silence, not knowing what to say and ashamed of their gentle feelings, for peasants are always ashamed of feeling refined, they finished eating and still sat hand in hand looking away into the distance. Everywhere the sowers were resting on little knolls, men, women and children sitting in silence. And the great calm of nature in spring filled the atmosphere around them. Everything seemed to sit still and wait until midday had passed. Only the gleaming sun chased westwards at a mighty pace, in and out through white clouds.

Then in a distant field an old man got up, took his spade and began to clean the earth from it with a piece of stone. The rasping noise carried a long way in the silence. That was the signal for a general rising all along the little valley. Young men stretched themselves and yawned. They walked slowly back to their ridges.

Martin's back and his wrists were getting a little sore, and Mary felt that if she stooped again over her seeds that her neck would break, but neither said anything and soon they had forgotten their tiredness in the mechanical movement of their bodies. The strong smell of the upturned earth acted like a drug on their nerves.

In the afternoon, when the sun was strongest, the old men of the village came out to look at their people sowing. Martin's grandfather, almost bent double over his thick stick, stopped in the land outside the field and, groaning loudly, leaned over the fence.

'God bless the work,' he called wheezily.

'And you, grandfather,' replied the couple together, but they did not stop working.

'Ha! ' muttered the old man to himself. 'Ha! He sows well and that woman is good too. They are beginning well.'

It was fifty years since he had begun with his Mary, full of hope and pride, and the merciless soil had hugged them to its bosom ever since, each spring, even by the aged who have spent their lives tilling the earth; so the old man, with his huge red nose and the spotted handkerchief tied around his skull under his black soft felt hat, watched his grandson work and gave him advice.

'Don't cut your sods so long,' he would wheeze, 'you are putting too much soil on your ridge.'

'Ah, woman! Don't plant a seed so near the edge. The stalk will come out sideways.'

And they paid no heed to him.

'Ah,' grumbled the old man, 'In my young days, when men worked from morning till night without tasting food, better work was done. But of course it can't be expected to be the same as it was. The breed is getting weaker. So it is.'

Then he began to cough in his chest and hobbled away to another field where his son Michael was working.

By sundown Martin had five ridges finished. He threw down his spade and stretched himself. All his bones ached and he wanted to lie down and rest. 'It's time to be going home, Mary,' he said.

Mary straightened herself, but she was too tired to reply. She looked at Martin wearily and it seemed to her that it was a great many years since they had set out that morning. Then she thought of the journey home and the trouble of feeding the pigs, putting the fowls into their coops and getting the supper ready and a momentary flash of rebellion against the slavery of being a peasant's wife crossed her mind. It passed in a moment. Martin was saying, as he dressed himself:

'Ha! My soul from the devil, it has been a good day's work. Five ridges done, and each one of them as straight as a steel rod. Begob, Mary it's no boasting to say that ye might well be proud of being the wife of Martin Delaney. And that's not saying the whole of it, my girl. You did your share better than any woman in Inverara could do it this blessed day.'

They stood for a few moments in silence looking at the work they had done. All her dissatisfaction and weariness vanished from Mary's mind with the delicious feeling of comfort that overcame her at having done this work with her husband. They had done it together. They had planted seeds in the earth. The next day and the next day and all their lives, when spring came they would have to bend their backs and do it until their hands and bones got twisted with rheumatism. But night would always bring sleep and forgetfulness.

As they walked home slowly Martin walked in front with another peasant talking about the sowing, and Mary walked behind, with her eyes on the ground, thinking.

Cows were lowing at a distance.

the letter
Líam O'Flaherty

IT WAS A SUMMER AFTERNOON. The clear blue sky was dotted with fluttering larks. The wind was still, as if it listened to their gentle singing. From the shining earth a faint smoke arose, like incense, shaken from invisible thuribles in a rhapsody of joy by hosts of unseen spirits. Such peace had fallen on the world! It seemed there was nothing but love and beauty everywhere; fragrant summer air and the laughter of happy birds. Everything listened to the singing larks in brooding thoughtlessness. Yea, even the horned snails lay stretched out on grey stones with their houses on their backs.

There was no loud sound. Nothing asserted its size in a brutal tumult of wind and thunder. Nothing swaggered with a raucous noise to disarrange the perfect harmony. Even the tiny insects mounting the blades of grass with slow feet were giants in themselves and things of pride to nature.

The grass blades, brushing with the movements of their growth, made joyous gentle sounds, like the sighs of a maiden in love.

A peasant and his family were working in a little field beneath the singing larks. The father, the mother and four children were there. They were putting fresh earth around sprouting potato stalks. They were very happy. It was a good thing to work there in the little field beneath the singing larks. Yes. God, maybe, gave music to cheer their simple hearts.

The mother and the second eldest daughter weeded the ridges, passing before the others. The father carefully spread around the stalks the precious clay that the eldest son dug from the rocky bottom of the shallow field. A younger son of twelve years, brought sea sand in a donkey's creels from a far corner of the field. They mixed the sand with the black clay. The fourth child, still almost an infant, staggered about near his mother, plucking weeds slowly and offering them to his mother as gifts.

They worked in silence; except once when by chance the father's shovel slipped on a stone and dislodged a young stalk from its shallow bed. The father uttered a cry. They all looked.

'Oh! Praised be God on high!' the mother said, crossing herself.

In the father's hands was the potato stalk and from its straggling thin roots there hung a cluster of tiny new potatoes, smaller than marbles. Already their seeds had borne fruit and multiplied. They all stood around and wondered. Then suddenly the eldest son, a stripling, spat on his hands and said wistfully:

'Ah! If Mary were here now wouldn't she be glad to see the new potatoes. I remember, on this very spot, she spread seaweed last winter.'

Silence followed this remark. It was of the eldest daughter he had spoken. She had gone to America in early spring. Since then they had only received one letter from her. A neighbour's daughter had written home recently, though, saying that Mary was without work. She had left her first place that a priest had found for her, as a servant in a rich woman's house.

The mother bowed her head and murmured sadly:

'God is good. Maybe to-day we'll get a letter.'

The father stooped again, struck the earth fiercely with his shovel and whispered harshly:

'Get on with the work.'

They moved away. But the eldest son mused for a while looking over the distant hills. Then he said loudly to his mother as if in defiance:

'It's too proud she is to write, mother, until she has money to send. I know Mary. She was always the proud one.'

They all bent over their work and the toddling child began again to bring weeds as gifts to his mother. The mother suddenly caught the child in her arms and kissed him. Then she said:

'Oh! They are like angels singing up there. Angels they are like. Wasn't God good to them to give them voices like that? Maybe if she heard the larks sing she'd write. But sure there are no larks in big cities.'

And nobody replied. But surely the larks no longer sang so happily. Now the sky became immense. The world became immense, an empty dangerous vastness. And the music of the fluttering birds had an eerie lilt to it. So they felt; all except the toddling child, who still came innocently to his mother, bringing little weeds as gifts.

Suddenly the merry cries of children mingled with the triumphant singing of the larks. They all paused and stood erect. Two little girls were running up the lane towards the field. Between the winding fences of the narrow lane they saw the darting white pinafores and the bobbing golden heads of the running girls. Their golden heads flashed in the sunlight. They came running, crying out joyously in trilling girlish voices. They were the two remaining children. They were coming home from school.

'What brought ye to the field?' the mother cried while they were still afar off.

'A letter,' one cried, as she jumped on to the fence of the field.

The father dropped his shovel and coughed. The mother crossed herself. The eldest son struck the ground with his spade and said: 'By the Book!'

'Yes, a letter from Mary,' said the other child, climbing over the fence also and eager to participate equally with her sister in the bringing of the good news. 'The postman gave it to us.'

They brought the letter to their father. All crowded round their father by the fence, where there was a little heap of stones.

The father sat down, rubbed his fingers carefully on his thighs and took the letter. They all knelt around his knees. The mother took the infant in her arms. They all became very silent. Their breathing became loud. The father turned the letter round about in his hands many times, examining it.

'It's her handwriting surely,' he said at length.

'Yes, yes,' said the eldest son. 'Open it, father.'

'In the name of God,' said the mother.

'God send us good news,' the father said, slowly tearing the envelope.

Then he paused again, afraid to look into the envelope. Then one of the girls said:

'Look, look. There's a cheque in it. I see it against the sun.'

'Eh?' said the mother.

With a rapid movement the father drew out the contents of the envelope. A cheque was within the folded letter. Not a word was spoken until he held up the cheque and said:

'Great God, it's for twenty pounds.'

'My darling,' the mother said, raising her eyes to the sky. 'My treasure, I bore you in my womb. My own sweet treasure.'

The children began to laugh, hysterical with joy. The father coughed and said in a low voice:

'There's a horse for that money to be had. A horse.'

'Oh! Father,' said the eldest son. 'A two-year-old and we'll break it on the strand. I'll break it, father. Then we'll have a horse like the people of the village. Isn't Mary great? Didn't I say she was waiting until she had money to send? A real horse!'

'And then I can have the ass for myself, daddy,' said the second boy.

And he yelled with joy.

'Be quiet will ye,' said the mother quietly in a sad tone. 'Isn't there a letter from my darling? Won't ye read me the letter?'

'Here,' said the father. 'Take it and read it one of ye. My hand is shaking.'

It was shaking and there were tears in his eyes, so that he could see nothing but a blur.

'I'll read it,' said the second daughter.

She took the letter, glanced over it from side to side and then suddenly burst into tears.

'What is it?' said the eldest son angrily. 'Give it to me.'

He took the letter, glanced over it and then his face became stern. All their faces became stern.

'Read it, son,' the father said.

' "Dear Parents," ' the son began. ' "Oh, mother, I am so lonely." It's all, all covered with blots same as if she were crying on the paper. "Daddy, why did I .... why did I ever ... ever ..." it's hard to make it out... yes... 'why did I ever come to this awful place? Say a prayer for me every night, mother. Kiss baby for me. Forgive me, mother. Your loving daughter Mary".'

When he finished there was utter silence for a long time. The father was the first to move. He rose slowly, still holding the cheque in his hand. Then he said:

'There was no word about the money in the letter,' he said in a queer voice. 'Why is that now?'

'Twenty pounds,' the mother said in a hollow voice. 'It isn't earned in a week.'

She snatched the letter furtively from her son and hid it ravenously in her bosom.

The father walked away slowly by the fence, whispering to himself in a dry voice:

'Aye! My greed stopped me asking myself that question. Twenty pounds.'

He walked away erect and stiff, like a man angrily drunk.

The others continued to sit about in silence, brooding. They no longer heard the larks. Suddenly one looked up and said in a frightened voice:

'What is father doing?'

They all looked. The father had passed out of the field into another uplying craggy field. He was now standing on a rock with his arms folded and his bare head fallen forward on his chest, perfectly motionless. His back was towards them but they knew he was crying. He had stood that way, apart, the year before, on the day their horse died.

Then the eldest son muttered a curse and jumped to his feet. He stood still with his teeth set and his wild eyes flashing. The infant boy dropped a weed from his tiny hands and burst into frenzied weeping.

Then the mother clutched the child in her arms and cried out in a despairing voice:

'Oh! Birds, birds, why do ye go on singing when my heart is frozen with grief.'

Together they all burst into a loud despairing wail and the harsh sound of their weeping rose into the sky from the field that had suddenly become ugly and lonely; up, up into the clear blue sky where the larks still sang their triumphant melody.

going into exile

liam o'flaherty

PATRICK FEENEY'S CABIN WAS CROWDED with people. In the large kitchen men, women and children lined the walls, three deep in places, sitting on forms, chairs, stools, and on one another's knees. On the cement floor three couples were dancing a jig and raising a quantity of dust, which was, however, soon sucked up the chimney by the huge turf fire that blazed on the hearth. The only clear space in the kitchen was the corner to the left of the fireplace, where Pat Mullaney sat on a yellow chair, with his right ankle resting on his left knee, a spotted red handkerchief on his head that reeked with perspiration, and his red face contorting as he played a tattered old accordian. One door was shut and the tins hanging on it gleamed in the firelight. The· opposite door was open and over the heads of the small boys that crowded in it and outside it, peering in at the dancing couples in the kitchen, a starry June sky was visible and, beneath the sky, shadowy grey crags and misty, whitish fields lay motionless, still and sombre. There was a deep, calm silence outside the cabin and within the cabin, in spite of the music and dancing in the kitchen, a starry June sky was visible and beneath the sky, Patrick Feeney's eldest son Michael sat on the bed with three other young men, there was a haunting melancholy in the air.

The people were dancing, laughing and singing with a certain forced and boisterous gaiety that failed to hide from them the real cause of their being there, dancing singing and laughing. For the dance was on account of Patrick Feeney's two children, Mary and Michael, who were going to the United States on the following morning.

Feeney himself, a black-bearded, red-faced, middle-aged

peasant, with white ivory buttons on his blue frieze shirt and his hands stuck in his leather waist belt, wandered restlessly about the kitchen, urging the people to sing and dance, while his mind was in agony all the time, thinking that on the following day he would lose his two eldest children, never to see them again perhaps. He kept talking to everybody about amusing things, shouted at the dancers and behaved in a boisterous and abandoned manner. But every now and then he had to leave the kitchen, under the pretence of going to the pigsty to look at a young pig that was supposed to be ill. He would stand, however, upright against his gable and look gloomily at some star or other, while his mind struggled with vague and peculiar ideas that wandered about in it. He could make nothing at all of his thoughts, but a lump always came up his throat, and he shivered although the night was warm.

Then he would sigh and say with a contraction of his neck: 'Oh, it's a queer world this and no doubt about it. So it is.' Then he would go back to the cabin again and begin to urge on the dance, laughing, shouting and stamping on the floor.

Towards dawn, when the floor was crowded with couples, arranged in fours, stamping on the floor and going to and fro, dancing the 'Walls of Limerick', Feeney was going out to the gable when his son Michael followed him out. The two of them walked side by side about the yard over the grey sea pebbles that had been strewn there the previous day. They walked in silence and yawned without need, pretending to be taking the air. But each of them was very excited. Michael was taller than his father and not so thickly built, but the shabby blue serge suit that he had bought for going to America was too narrow for his broad shoulders and the coat was too wide around the waist. He moved clumsily in it and his hands appeared altogether too bony and big and red, and he didn't know what to do with them. During his twenty-one years of life he had never worn anything other than the homespun clothes of Inverara, and the shop-made clothes appeared as strange to him and as uncomfortable as a dress suit worn by a man working in a sewer. His face was flushed a bright red and his blue eyes shone with excitement. Now and again he wiped the perspiration from his forehead with the lining of his grey tweed cap.

At last Patrick Feeney reached his usual position at the gable end. He halted, balanced himself on his heels with his hands in his waist belt, coughed and said, 'It's going to be a warm day.' The son came up beside him, folded his arms and leaned his right shoulder against the gable.

'It was kind of Uncle Ned to lend the money for the dance, father,' he said. 'I'd hate to think that we'd have to go without something or other, just the same as everybody else has. I'll send you that money, the very first money I earn, father... even before I pay Aunt Mary for my passage money. I should have all that money paid off in four months, and then I'll have some more money to send you by Christmas.'

And Michael felt very strong and manly recounting what he was going to do when he got to Boston, Massachusetts. He told himself that with his great strength he would earn a great deal of money. Conscious of his youth and his strength and lusting for adventurous life, for the moment he forgot the ache in his heart that the thought of leaving his father inspired in him.

The father was silent for some time. He was looking at the sky with his lower lip hanging, thinking of nothing. At last he sighed as a memory struck him. 'What is it?' said the son. 'Don't weaken, for God's sake. You will only make it hard for me.' 'Fooh! said the father suddenly with pretended gruffness. 'Who is weakening? I'm afraid that your new clothes make you impudent.' Then he was silent for a moment and continued in a low voice: 'I was thinking of that potato field you sowed alone last spring the time I had influenza. I never set eyes on the man that could do it better. It's a cruel world that takes you away from the land that God made you for.'

'Oh, what are you talking about, father?' said Michael irritably. 'Sure what did anybody ever get out of the land but poverty and hard work and potatoes and salt?'

'Ah yes,' said the father with a sigh, 'but it's your own, the land, and over there' – he waved his hand at the western sky – 'you'll be giving your sweat to some other man's land, or what's equal to it.'

'Indeed,' muttered Michael looking at the ground with a melancholy expression in his eyes. 'It's poor encouragement you are giving me.'

They stood in silence fully five minutes. Each hungered to embrace the other, to cry, to beat the air, to scream with excess of sorrow. But they stood silent and sombre, like nature about them, hugging their woe. Then they went back to the cabin. Michael went into the little room to the left of the kitchen, to the three young men who fished in the same curragh with him and were his bosom friends. The father walked into the large bedroom to the right of the kitchen.

The large bedroom was also crowded with people. A large table was laid for tea in the centre of the room and about a dozen young men were sitting at it, drinking tea and eating buttered raisin cake. Mrs. Feeney was bustling about the table, serving the food and urging them to eat. She was assisted by her two younger daughters and by another woman, a relative of her own. Her eldest daughter Mary, who was going to the United States that day, was sitting on the edge of the bed with several other young women. The bed was a large four poster bed with a deal canopy over it, painted red, and the young women were huddled together on it. So that there must have been about a dozen of them there. They were Mary Feeney's particular friends, and they stayed with her in that uncomfortable position just to show how much they liked her. It was a custom.

Mary herself sat on the edge of the bed with her legs dangling. She was a pretty, dark-haired girl of nineteen, with dimpled, plump, red cheeks and ruminative brown eyes that seemed to cause little wrinkles to come and go in her low forehead. Her nose was soft and small and rounded. Her mouth was small and the lips were red and open. Beneath her white blouse that was frilled at the neck and her navy blue skirt that outlined her limbs as she sat on the edge of the bed, her body was plump, soft, well-moulded and in some manner exuded a feeling of freshness and innocence. So that she seemed to have been born to be fondled and admired in luxurious surroundings instead of having been born a peasant's daughter, who had to go to the United States that day to work as a servant or maybe in a factory.

As she sat on the edge of the bed crushing her little handkerchief between her palms, she kept thinking feverishly of the United States, at one moment with fear and loathing, at the next with desire and longing. Unlike her brother she did not think of the work she was going to do or the money that she was going to earn. Other things troubled her, things of which she was half ashamed, half afraid, thoughts of love and of foreign men and of clothes and of houses where there were more than three rooms and where people ate meat every day. She was fond of life, and several young men among the local gentry had admired her in Inverara. But...

She happened to look up and she caught her father's eyes as he stood silently by the window with his hands stuck in his waist belt. His eyes rested on hers for a moment and then he dropped them without smiling, and with his lips compressed he walked down into the kitchen. She shuddered slightly. She was a little afraid of her father, although she knew that he loved her very much and he was very kind to her. But the winter before he had whipped her with a dried willow rod, when he caught her one evening behind Tim Hernon's cabin after nightfall, with Tim Hernon's son Bartly's arms around her waist and he kissing her. Ever since, she always shivered slightly when her father touched her or spoke to her.

'Oho!' said an old peasant who sat at the table with a saucer full of tea in his hand and his grey flannel shirt open at his thin, hairy, wrinkled neck. 'Oho! indeed, but it's a disgrace to the island of Inverara to let such a beautiful woman as your daughter go away, Mrs. Feeney. If I were a young man, I'd be flayed alive if I'd let her go.'

There was a laugh and some of the women on the bed said: 'Bad cess to you, Patsy Coyne, if you haven't too much impudence, it's a caution.' But the laugh soon died. The young men sitting at the table felt embarrassed and kept looking at one another sheepishly, as if each tried to find out if the others were in love with Mary Feeney.

'Oh, well, God is good,' said Mrs. Feeney, as she wiped her lips with the tip of her bright, clean, check apron. 'What will be must be, and sure there is hope from the sea, but there is no hope from the grave. It is sad and the poor have to suffer, but...' Mrs. Feeney stopped suddenly, aware that all these platitudes meant nothing whatsoever. Like her husband she was unable to think intelligently about her two children going away. Whenever the reality of their going away, maybe for ever, three thousand miles into a vast unknown world, came before her mind, it seemed that a thin bar of some hard metal thrust itself forward from her brain and rested behind the wall of her forehead. So that almost immediately she became stupidly conscious of the pain caused by the imaginary bar of metal and she forgot the dread prospect of her children going away. But her mind grappled with the things about her busily and efficiently, with the preparation of food, with the entertaining of her guests, with the numerous little things that have to be done in a house where there is a party and which only a woman can do properly. These little things, in a manner, saved her, for the moment at least, from bursting into tears whenever she looked at her daughter and whenever she thought of her son, whom she loved most of all her children, because perhaps she nearly died giving birth to him and he had been very delicate until he was twelve years old. So she laughed down in her breast a funny laugh she had that made her heave when her check apron rose out from the waist band in a deep curve. 'A person begins to talk,' she said with a shrug of her shoulders sideways, 'and then a person says foolish things.'

'That's true,' said the old peasant, noisily pouring more tea from his cup to his saucer.

But Mary knew by her mother laughing that way that she was very near being hysterical. She always laughed that way before she had one of her fits of hysterics. And Mary's heart stopped beating suddenly and then began again at an awful rate as her eyes became acutely conscious of her mother's body, the rotund, short body with the wonderful mass of fair hair growing grey at the temples and the fair face with the soft liquid brown eyes, that grew hard and piercing for a moment as they looked at a thing and then grew soft and liquid again, and the thin-lipped small mouth with the beautiful white teeth and the deep perpendicular grooves in the upper lip and the tremor that always came in the corner of the mouth, with love, when she looked at the children. Mary became acutely conscious of all these little points, as well as of the little black spot that was on her left breast below the nipple and the swelling that came now and again in her legs and caused her to have hysterics and would one day cause her death. And she was stricken with horror at the thought of leaving her mother and at the selfishness of her thoughts. She had never been prone to thinking of anything important but now, somehow for a moment, she had a glimpse of her mother's life that made her shiver and hate herself as a cruel, heartless, lazy, selfish wretch. Her mother's life loomed up before her eyes, a life of continual misery and suffering, hard work, birth pangs, sickness and again hard work and hunger and anxiety. It loomed up and then it fled again, a little mist came before her eyes and she jumped down from the bed, with the jaunty twirl of her head that was her habit when she set her body in motion.

'Sit down for a while, mother,' she whispered, toying with one of the black ivory buttons on her mother's brown bodice. 'I'll look after the table.' 'No, no,' murmured the mother with a shake of her whole body, 'I'm not a bit tired. Sit down, my treasure. You have a long way to travel to-day.'

And Mary sighed and went back to the bed again.

At last somebody said: 'It's broad daylight.' And immediately everybody looked out and said: 'So it is, and may God be praised.' The change from the starry night to the grey, sharp dawn, was hard to notice until it had arrived. People looked out and saw the morning light sneaking over the crags, silently, along the ground, pushing the mist banks upwards. The stars were growing dim. A long way off invisible sparrows were chirping in their ivied perch in some distant hill or other. Another day had arrived and even as the people looked at it, yawned and began to search for their hats, caps and shawls preparing to go home, the day grew and spread its light and made things move and give voice. Cocks crew, blackbirds carolled, a dog let loose from a cabin by an early riser chased madly after an imaginary robber, barking as if his tail were on fire. The people said goodbye and began to stream forth from Feeney's cabin. They were going to their homes to see to the morning's work before going to Kilmurrage to see the emigrants off on the steamer to the mainland. Soon the cabin was empty except for the family.

All the family gathered into the kitchen and stood about for some minutes talking sleepily of the dance and of the people who had been present. Mrs. Feeney tried to persuade everybody to go to bed, but everybody refused. It was four o'clock and Michael and Mary would have to set out for Kilmurrage at nine. So tea was made and they all sat about for an hour drinking it and eating rasin cake and talking. They only talked of the dance and of the people who had been present.

There were eight of them there, the father and mother and six children. The youngest child was Thomas, a thin boy of twelve, whose lungs made a singing sound every time he breathed. The next was Bridget, a girl of fourteen, with dancing eyes and a habit of shaking her short golden curls every now and then for no apparent reason. Then there were the twins, Julia and Margaret, quiet, rather stupid, flat-faced girls of sixteen. Both their upper front teeth protruded slightly and they were both great workers and very obedient to their mother. They were all sitting at the table, having just finished a third large pot of tea, when suddenly the mother hastily gulped down the remainder of the tea in her cup, dropped the cup with a clatter to her saucer and sobbed once through her nose.

'Now mother,' said Michael sternly, 'what's the good of this work?'

'No, you are right, my pulse,' she replied quietly. 'Only I was just thinking how nice it is to sit here surrounded by all my children, all my little birds in my nest, and then two of them going to fly away made me sad.' And she laughed, pretending to treat it as a foolish joke.

'Oh, that be damned for a story,' said the father, wiping his mouth on his sleeve; 'there's work to be done. You Julia, go and get the horse. Margaret, you milk the cow and see that you give enough milk to the calf this morning.' And he ordered everybody about as if it were an ordinary day of work.

But Michael and Mary had nothing to do and they sat about miserably conscious that they had cut adrift from the routine of their home life. They no longer had any place in it. In a few hours they would be homeless wanderers. Now that they were cut adrift from it, the poverty and sordidness of their home life appeared to them under the aspect of comfort and plenty.

So the morning passed until breakfast time at seven o'clock. The morning's work was finished and the family was gathered together again. The meal passed in a dead silence. Drowsy after the sleepless night and conscious that the parting would come in a few hours, nobody wanted to talk. Everybody had an egg for breakfast in honour of the occasion. Mrs. Feeney, after her usual habit, tried to give her egg first to Michael, then to Mary, and as each refused it, she ate a little herself and gave the remainder to little Thomas who had the singing in his chest. Then the breakfast was cleared away. The father went to put the creels on the mare so as to take the luggage into Kilmurrage. Michael and Mary got the luggage ready and began to get dressed. The mother and the other children tidied up the house. People from the village began to come into the kitchen, as was customary, in order to accompany the emigrants from their home to Kilmurrage.

At last everything was ready. Mrs. Feeney had exhausted all excuses for moving about, engaged on trivial tasks. She had to go into the big bedroom where Mary was putting on her new hat. The mother sat on a chair by the window, her face contorting on account of the flood of tears she was keeping back. Michael moved about the room uneasily, his two hands knotting a big red handkerchief behind his back. Mary twisted about in front of the mirror that hung over the black wooden mantlepiece. She was spending a long time with the hat. It was the first one she had ever worn, but it fitted her beautifully, and it was in excellent taste. It was given to her by the schoolmistress, who was very fond of her, and she herself had taken it in a little. She had an instinct for beauty in dress and deportment.

But the mother, looking at how well her daughter wore the cheap navy blue costume and the white frilled blouse, and the little round black hat with a fat, fluffy, glossy curl covering each ear, and the black silk stockings with blue clocks in them, and the little black shoes that had laces of three colours in them, got suddenly enraged with... She didn't know with what she got enraged. But for the moment she hated her daughter's beauty, and she remembered all the anguish of giving birth to her and nursing her and toiling for her, for no other purpose than to lose her now and let her go away, maybe to be ravished wantonly because of her beauty and her love of gaiety. A cloud of mad jealousy and hatred against this impersonal beauty that she saw in her daughter almost suffocated the mother, and she stretched out her hands in front of her unconsciously and then just as suddenly her anger vanished like a puff of smoke, and she burst into wild tears, wailing: 'My children, oh, my children, far over the sea you will be carried from me, your mother.' And she began to rock herself and she threw her apron over her head.

Immediately the cabin was full of the sound of bitter wailing. A dismal cry rose from the women gathered in the kitchen. 'Far over the sea they will be carried,' began woman after woman, and then they all rocked themselves and hid their heads in their aprons. Michael's mongrel dog began to howl on the hearth. Little Thomas sat down on the hearth beside the dog, and putting his arms around him, he began to cry, although he didn't know exactly why he was crying, but he felt melancholy on account of the dog howling and so many people being about.

In the bedroom the son and daughter, on their knees, clung to their mother, who held their heads between her hands and rained kisses on both heads ravenously. After the first wave of tears she had stopped weeping. The tears still ran down her cheeks, but her eyes gleamed and they were dry. There was a fierce look in them as she searched all over the heads of her two children with them, with her brows contracted, searching with a fierce terror-stricken expression, as if by the intensity of her stare she hoped to keep a living photograph of them before her mind. With her quivering lips she made a queer sound like 'im-m-m-m' and she kept kissing. Her right hand clutched at Mary's left shoulder and with her left she fondled the back of Michael's neck. The two children were sobbing freely. They must have stayed that way a quarter of an hour.

Then the father came into the room, dressed in his best clothes.

He wore a new frieze waistcoat, with a grey and black front and a white back. He held his soft black felt hat in one hand and in the other hand he had a bottle of holy water. He coughed and said in a weak gentle voice that was strange to him, as he touched his son: 'Come now, it is time.'

Mary and Michael got to their feet. The father sprinkled them with holy water and they crossed themselves. Then, without looking at their mother, who lay in the chair with her hands clasped on her lap, looking at the ground in a silent tearless stupor, they left the room. Each hurriedly kissed little Thomas, who was not going to Kilmurrage, and then, hand in hand, they left the house. As Michael was going out the door he picked a piece of loose whitewash from the wall and put it in his pocket. The people filed out after them, down the yard and on to the road, like a funeral procession. The mother was left in the house with little Thomas and two old peasant women from the village. Nobody spoke in the cabin for a long time.

Then the mother rose and came into the kitchen. She looked at the two women, at her little son and at the hearth, as if she were looking for something she had lost. Then she threw her hands into the air and ran out into the yard.

'Come back,' she screamed; 'come back to me.'

She looked wildly down the road with dilated nostrils, her bosom heaving. But there was nobody in sight. Nobody replied. There was a crooked stretch of limestone road, surrounded by grey crags that were scorched by the sun. The road ended in a hill and then dropped out of sight. The hot June day was silent. Listening foolishly for an answering cry, the mother imagined she could hear the crags simmering under the hot rays of the sun. It was something in her head that was singing.

The two old women led her back into the kitchen. 'There is nothing that time will not cure,' said one. 'Yes. Time and patience,' said the other.

the test of courage

Liam O'Flaherty

AT SUNDOWN on a summer evening Michael O'Hara and Peter Cooke left their village with great secrecy. Crouching behind fences, they made a wide circuit and then ran all the way to a little rock-bound harbour that lay a mile to the southwest. They carried their caps in their hands as they ran and they panted with excitement. They were about to execute a plan of adventure which they had devised for weeks. They were going to take Jimmy the weaver's boat out for a night's bream fishing.

Michael O'Hara was twelve years and four months, five months younger than his comrade. He had very intelligent eyes of a deep-blue colour and his fair hair stood up on end like close-cropped bristles. He looked slender and rather delicate in his blue jersey and grey flannel trousers that only reached half-way down his bare shins. Although it was he who had conceived and planned the adventure, just as he planned all the adventures of the two comrades, he now lagged far behind in the race for the port. This was partly due to his inferior speed. It was also due to a nervous reaction against embarking on an expedition that would cause grave anxiety to his parents.

Peter Cooke looked back after reaching the great mound of boulders that lined the head of the harbour. He frowned and halted when he saw his companion far behind. His sturdy body seemed to be too large for his clothes, which were identical with those worn by O'Hara. His hair was black and curly. His face was freckled. He had the heavy jaws and thick nose of a fighter. His small grey eyes, set close together, lacked the intelligence of Michael O'Hara's eyes.

'Hurry on,' he cried in a loud whisper, when Michael came

closer, 'What ails you? Are you tired already?'

Michael looked back over his shoulder furtively.

'I thought I saw somebody,' he said in a nervous tone.

'Who?' said Peter. 'Who did you see?'

'Over there,' Michael said.

He pointed towards the north in the direction of the village, which was now half hidden by the intervening land. Only the thatched roofs and the smoking chimneys of the houses were visible. The smoke rose straight up from the chimneys in the still twilight. To the west of the village ran a lane, its low fence standing out against the fading horizon of the sky like a curtain full of irregular holes.

'I think it was my mother I saw coming home from milking the cow along the lane,' Michael said in a voice that was slightly regretful. 'I just saw her head over the fence, but it looked like her shawl. I don't think she saw me, though. Even if she did see me, she wouldn't know who it was.'

'Come on,' Peter said. 'She couldn't see you that far away. We have to hurry or it will be dark before we get that curragh in the water.'

As nimbly as goats, the two boys ran down the sloping mound of granite boulders and along the flat stretch of grey limestone that reached out to the limit of the tide. Then they went into a cave beneath a low cliff that bordered the shore. They brought the gear they had hidden in this cave down to the sea's edge and dropped it at the point where they were to launch the boat.

'Do you think we'll be able to carry her down, Peter?' Michael said, as they ran back across the mound of boulders to fetch the boat.

Peter halted suddenly and looked at his comrade. He was irritated by the nervous tone of Michael's voice.

'Are you getting afraid?' he said roughly.

'Who? Me?' said Michael indignantly.

'If you are,' said Peter, 'say the word and we'll go back home. I don't want to go out with you if you start whinging.'

'Who's whinging?' said Michael. 'I only thought we mightn't be able to carry her down to the rock. Is there any harm in that?'

'Come on,' said Peter, 'and stop talking nonsense. Didn't we get under her four times to see could we raise her? We raised her, didn't we? If we could raise her, we can carry her. Jimmy the weaver can rise under her all by himself and he's an old man. He's such a weak old man, too, that no crew in the village would take him out fishing with them. It would be a shame if the two of us weren't as strong as Jimmy the weaver.'

'I hope he won't put a curse on us,' Michael said as they walked along, 'when he finds out that we took his curragh. He's terrible for cursing when he gets angry. I've seen him go on his two knees and curse when two eggs were stolen from under his goose and she hatching. He pulled up his trousers and cursed on his naked knees.'

'He'd be an ungrateful man,' Peter said, 'if he put a curse on us after all we've done for him during the past week. Four times we drew water from the well for him. We dug potatoes for him in his little garden twice and we gave him a rabbit that we caught. The whole village would throw stones at his house if he put a curse on us after we doing all that for him.'

All the village boats usually rested on the flat ground behind the mound of granite boulders. There was a little wall of loose stones around each boat to protect it from the great south winds that sometimes blew in from the ocean. At present only the weaver's boat remained in its stone pen, lying bottom up within its protecting wall, with stone props under the transoms to keep it from the ground. All the other pens were empty, for it was the height of the bream season and the men were at sea.

'Come on now,' Peter said when they reached the boat. 'Lift up the bow.'

They got on each side of the bow and raised it without difficulty.

'You get under it now and settle yourself,' Peter said. Michael crouched and got under the boat, with his face towards the stern. He rested his shoulders against the front seat and braced his elbows against the frame.

Although they had practised raising the boat, he now began to tremble lest he might not be able to bear the weight when Peter raised the stern.

'Keep your legs well apart' Peter said, 'and stand loose same as I told you.'

'I'm ready,' Michael said nervously. 'You go ahead and raise her.'

Peter put on his cap with the peak turned backwards, then he set himself squarely under the stern of the boat. He gritted his teeth and made his strong back rigid. Then he drew in a deep breath and made a sudden effort.

He raised the boat and then spread his legs to distribute the weight. Both boys staggered for a few moments, as they received the full weight of the boat on their shoulders.

'Are you balanced?' Peter said.

'Go ahead,' said Michael.

Peter led the way, advancing slowly with the rhythmic movement of his body which he had copied from his elders. He held his body rigid above the hips, which swayed as he threw his legs forward limply in an outward arc. As each foot touched the ground, he lowered his hips and then raised them again with the shifting of weight to the other foot.

Michael tried to imitate this movement, but he was unable to do it well owing to his nervousness. In practice he had been just as good as Peter. Now, however, the memory of his mother's shawled head kept coming into his mind to disturb him.

'Try to keep in step,' Peter called out, 'and don't grip the frame. Let your shoulders go dead.'

'I'm doing my best,' Michael said, 'but it keeps shifting on my shoulders.'

'That's because you're taking a grip with your hands. Let your shoulders go dead.'

They were both exhausted when they finally laid down the boat on the weed-covered rock by the sea's edge. They had to rest a little while. Then they gently pushed the boat into the water over the smooth carpet of red weed. They had to do this very carefully, because the coracle was just a light frame of thin pine lathes covered with tarred canvas. The least contact with a sliver of stone or even with a limpet cone, could have put a hole in the canvas. Fortunately the sea was dead calm, and they managed the launching without accident.

'Now, in God's name,' Peter said, imitating a man's voice as he dipped his hand in the seawater and made the sign of the Cross on his forehead according to ritual, 'I'll go aboard and put her under way. You hand in the gear when I bring her stern to shore.'

He got into the prow seat, unshipped the oars and dipped the glambs in the water before fixing them on the thole pins. Then he manoeuvred the stern of the boat face to the rock. Michael threw aboard the gear, which included a can of half-baited limpets for bait, four lines coiled on small wooden frames, half a loaf of bread rolled up in a piece of cloth, and the anchor rope with a large granite stone attached. Then he also dipped his right hand in the brine water and made the sign of the Cross on his forehead.

'In God's name,' he said reverently, as he put one knee on the stern and pushed against the rock with his foot, 'head her out.'

As Peter began to row, Michael took his seat on the after transom and unshipped his oars. He dipped the glambs in the water and put the oars on the thole pins.

'Face land, right hand underneath,' Peter called out just like a grown-up captain giving orders to his crew.

'I'm with you,' Michael said. 'Head her out.'

The two boys rowed well, keeping time perfectly. Soon they had cleared the mouth of the little harbour and they were in the open sea. Night was falling, but they could see the dark cluster of village boats beneath a high cliff to the west. They turned east.

'Take a mark now and keep her straight,' Peter said.

Michael brought two points on the dim land to the west into line with the stern and they rowed eastwards until they came abreast of a great pile of rock that had fallen from the cliff. Here they cast anchor. When they had tied the anchor rope to the cross-stick in the bow, the boat swung round and became motionless on the still water.

'Oh!, You devil!' Peter said excitedly. 'Out with the lines now and let us fish. Wouldn't it be wonderful if we caught a boat load of bream. We'd be the talk of the whole parish.'

'Maybe we will,' cried Michael, equally excited.

Now he was undisturbed by the memory of his mother's shawled head. Nor was he nervous about his position, out at night on a treacherous ocean in a frail coracle. The wild rapture of adventure had taken full possession of him.

Such was the haste with which they baited and paid out their lines that they almost transfixed their hands with the hooks. Each boy paid out two lines, one on either side of the boat. They had cast anchor right in the midst of a school of bream. Peter was the first to get his lines into water. They had barely sunk when he got a strike on both of them.

'Oh! You devil! he cried. 'I've got two.'

In his excitement he tried to haul the two lines simultaneously and lost both of the soft-lipped fish. In the meantime, Michael also got a strike on one of his lines. He swallowed his breath and hauled rapidly. A second fish struck while he was hauling the first line. He also became greedy and grabbed the second line letting the first fish escape. But he landed the second fish.

'Oh! Peter, he cried, 'we'll fill the boat like you said.'

He put the fish smartly between his knees and pulled the hook from its mouth. He dropped it on the bottom of the boat, where it began to beat a tattoo with its tail.

'Oh! You Devil! Peter cried. 'The sea is full of them.'

He had again thrown his lines into the water and two fish immediately impaled themselves on the hooks. This time he landed both fish, as the lessening of excitement enabled him to use his skill.

'We should have brought more limpets,' Michael said, 'This lot we brought won't be half enough!'

The fish continued to strike. Despite losing a large percentage, they had caught thirty-five before an accident drove the boat away from the school. A light breeze had come up from the land. It hardly made a ripple on the surface of the sea, yet its impact caused the boat to lean away from the restraint of the anchor rope. The rope went taught. Then the anchor stone slipped from the edge of a reef on which it had dropped. Falling into deeper water, it could not find ground. The boat swung round and began to drift straight out to sea, pressed by the gentle breeze. The two boys, intent on their fishing, did not notice the accident. Soon, however, the fish ceased to strike. They did not follow the boat into deep water. The lines hung idly over the sides.

'They're gone, Michael said. 'Do you think it's time for us to go home?'

'We can't go home yet,' Peter said indignantly. 'We have only thirty-five fish yet. Wait until they begin to strike again when the tide turns. Then you'll see that we'll fill the boat. In any case, we can't go back until the moon rises. It's too dark now to make our way past the reef.'

'It's dark all right,' Michael said in a low voice. 'I can't see land, though it's so near.'

Now that the fish had gone away, the vision of his mother's shawled head returned to prick his conscience, and the darkness frightened him as it always did. Yet he dared not insist on trying to make port, lest Peter might think he was a coward.

'They'll start biting again, Peter continued eagerly. 'You wait and see. We'll fill the boat. Then the moon will be up and it will be lovely rowing into port. Won't they be surprised when they see all the fish we have? They won't say a word to us when we bring home that awful lot of fish.

Michael shuddered on being reminded of the meeting with his parents after his escapade.

'I'm hungry,' he said. 'Do you think we should eat our bread?

No use bringing it back home again.'

'I'm hungry, too,' Peter said. 'Let's eat the bread while we're waiting for the tide to turn.'

They divided the half loaf and began to eat ravenously. When they had finished, Michael felt cold and sleepy.

'We should have brought more clothes to put on us,' he said. 'The sea gets awful cold at night, doesn't it?'

'Let's lie up in the bow,' Peter said, 'I feel cold myself. We'll lie together in the shelter of the bow while we're waiting for the tide to turn. That way we won't feel the cold in the shelter of the bow.'

They lay down in the bow side by side. There was just room enough for their two bodies stretched close together.

'It's much warmer this way sure enough,' Michael said sleepily.

'It's just like being in bed,' Peter said, 'Oh! You Devil! When I grow up I'll be a sailor. Then I can sleep every night out in the middle of the sea.'

They fell asleep almost at once. In their sleep they put their arms about one another. The moon rose and its eerie light fell on them, as they lay asleep in the narrow bow rocked gently by the boat's movement, to the soft music of the lapping water. The moonlight fell on the dark sides of the boat that drifted before the breeze. It shone on the drifting lines that hung from the black sides, like the tentacles of an evil monster that was carrying the sleeping boys out far over the empty ocean.

The dead fish were covered with a phosphorescent glow when the boat swayed towards the moon.

Then the moonlight faded and dawn came over the sea. The sun rose in the east and its rays began to dance on the black canvas. Michael was the first to awaken. He uttered a cry of fright when he looked about him and discovered where he was. The land was now a great distance. It was little more than a dot on the far horizon. He gripped Peter by the head with both hands.

'Wake up, Peter, he cried. 'Oh! Wake up. Something terrible has happened.'

Thinking he was at home in bed, Peter tried to push Michael away and to turn over on his other side.

'It's not time to get up yet,' he muttered.

When he finally was roused and realized what had happened, he was much more frightened than Michael.

'Oh! You Devil!' he said. 'we pulled anchor. We're lost.'

There was a look of ignorant panic in his small eyes. Michael bit his lip, in an effort to keep himself from crying out loud. It was a great shock to find that Peter, who had always been the leader of the two comrades and who had never before shown any signs of fear, was now in panic.

'We're not lost,' he said angrily. 'Will you look where the land is?' cried Peter. 'Will you look?'

Suddenly Michael felt that he no longer wanted to cry. His eyes got a hard and almost cruel expression in them.

'Stand up, will you?' he said sharply. 'Let me pull the rope.'

Peter looked at Michael stupidly and got out of the way. He sat on the forward transom, while Michael hauled in the anchor rope.

'What could we do?' he said. 'We're lost unless they come and find us. We could never row that far with the wind against us.'

'Why don't you give me a hand with the rope and stop whinging?' cried Michael angrily.

Peter was roused by this insult from a boy whom he had until now been able to dominate. He glared at Michael, spat on his hands and jumped to his feet.

'Get out of my way,' he said gruffly. 'Give me a hold of that rope. Look who's talking about whinging.'

With his superior strength, Peter quickly got the rope and anchor stone into the bow. Then the two of them hauled in the lines. They did not trouble to wind them on the frames but left them lying in a tangled heap on the bottom.

'Hurry up' Peter kept saying. 'We have to hurry out of here.' Still roused to anger by Michael's insult, he got out his oars and turned the bow towards the dot of land on the horizon. Michael also got out his oars.

'Left hand on top,' Peter shouted, 'and give it your strength. Stretch to it. Stretch.'

'We better take it easy, Michael said. 'We have a long way to go.'

'Stretch to it, I tell you,' Peter shouted still more loudly. 'Give it your strength if you have any.'

As soon as he found the oars in his hands, as a means of escape from what he feared, he allowed himself again to go into a panic. He rowed wildly, leaping from the transom with each stroke.

'Why can't you keep time?' Michael shouted at him.

'Keep time with the stern. You'll only kill yourself that way.'

'Row you devil and stop talking,' cried Peter. 'Give length to your stroke and you'll be able to row with me.'

'But you're supposed to keep with me' Michael said. 'You're supposed to keep with the stern.'

Suddenly Peter pulled so hard that he fell right back off the transom of the bow. One of the oars jumped off the thole pin as he fell backwards. It dropped over the side of the boat and began to drift astern. Michael turned the boat and picked up the oar.

'Don't do that again, he said as he gave the oar to Peter. 'Listen to what I tell you and row quietly.'

Peter looked in astonishment at the cruel eyes of his comrade. He was now completely dominated by them.

'It's no use, Michael,' he said dejectedly. 'You see the land is as far away as ever. It's no use trying to row.'

'We'll make headway if we row quietly,' Michael said. 'Come on now. Keep time with the stern.'

Now that he had surrendered to the will of his comrade Peter rowed obediently in time with the stern oars. The boat began to make good way.

'That's better,' Michael said, when they had been rowing a little while. 'They'll soon be out looking for us,' said Peter. 'Sure nobody saw us leave the port'.

'They'll see the boat is gone,' Michael said. 'Why can't you have sense? I bet they're out looking for us now. All we have to do is to keep rowing quietly.'

'And how would they see us?' Peter said after a pause. 'We can hardly see that land from here, even though it's so big. How could they see this curragh from the land and it no bigger than a thimble on the water?'

Michael suddenly raised his voice and said angrily: 'Is it how you want us to lie down and let her drift away until we die of hunger and thirst? Stop talking and row quietly. You'll only tire yourself out with your talk.'

'Don't you be shouting at me, Michael O'Hara.' Peter cried. 'You better watch out for yourself. Is it how you think I'm afraid of you?'

They rowed in silence after that for more than two hours. The boat made good way and the land became much more distinct on the horizon. It kept rising up from the ocean and assuming its normal shape. Then Peter dropped his oars and let his head hang forward on his chest. Michael went forward to him.

'I'm thirsty' Peter said. 'I'm dying with the thirst. Is there any sign of anybody coming?'

'There is no sign yet, Peter,' Michael said gently. 'We have to have courage, though. They'll come all right. Let you lie down in the bow for a while. I'll put your jersey over your face to keep the sun from touching you. That way you won't feel the thirst so much, I heard my father say so.'

He had to help Peter into the bow, as the older boy was completely helpless with exhaustion. He pulled off Peter's jersey and put it over his face.

'Lie there for a while' he said, 'and I'll keep her from drifting. Then you can spell me.'

He returned to his seat and continued to row. He suffered terribly from thirst. He was also beginning to feel the first pangs of sea-hunger. Yet he experienced an exaltation that made him impervious to this torture. Ever since his imagination had begun to develop, he had been plagued by the fear that he would not be able to meet danger with courage. Even though he deliberately sought out little dangers and tested himself against them without flinching, he continued to believe that the nervousness he felt on these occasions was a sign of cowardice and that he would fail when the big test came.

Now that the big test had come, he experienced the first dark rapture of manhood instead of fear. His blue eyes were no longer soft and dreamy. They had a look of sombre cruelty in them, the calm arrogance of the fighting male. His mind was at peace, because he was now free from the enemy that had lurked within him. Even the pain in his bowels and in his parched throat only served to excite the triumphant will of his awakening manhood. When his tired muscles could hardly clutch the oars within his blistered palms, he still continued to row mechanically.

In the afternoon, when the village boats finally came to the rescue, Michael was still sitting on his transom, trying to row feebly. By then he was so exhausted that he did not hear the approach of the boats until a man shouted from the nearest one of them. Hearing the shout he fell from his seat in a faint.

When he recovered consciousness, he was in the bow of his father's boat. His father was holding a bottle of water to his lips. He looked up into his father's rugged face and smiled when he saw there was no anger in it. On the contrary, he had never before seen such tenderness in his father's stern eyes.

'Was it how you dragged anchor?' his father said.

Although his upper lip was twitching with emotion, he spoke in a casual tone, as to a comrade.

'It could happen to the best of men,' the father continued

thoughtfully after Michael had nodded his head. 'There's no harm done though, thank God.'

He put some clothes under the boy's head, caressed him roughly and told him to go to sleep. Michael closed his eyes. In another boat, Peter's father was shouting in an angry tone.

Michael opened his eyes again when his father and the other men in the boat had begun to row. He looked at the muscular back of his father, who was rowing in the bow seat. A wave of ardent love for his father swept through his blood, making him feel tender and weak. Tears began to stream from his eyes, but they were tears of joy because his father had looked at him with tenderness and spoken to him as to a comrade.

Riders to the Sea

J. M. Synge

PERSONS IN THE PLAY

MAURYA, *an old woman*
BARTLEY, *her son*
CATHLEEN, *her daughter*
NORA, *a younger daughter*
MEN AND WOMEN

SCENE – *An island off the West of Ireland*

Cottage kitchen, with nets, oilskins, spinning-wheel, some new boards standing by the wall, etc. Cathleen, a girl of about twenty finishes kneading cake, and puts it down in the pot-oven by the fire; then wipes her hands, and begins to spin at the wheel. Nora, a young girl, puts her head in at the door.

Nora *(in a low voice).* Where is she?

Cathleen. She's lying down, God help her, and maybe sleeping, if she's able.

Nora *comes in softly, and takes a bundle from under her shawl.*

Cathleen *(spinning the wheel rapidly).* What is it you have?

Nora. The young priest is after bringing them. It's a shirt and a plain stocking were got off a drowned man in Donegal.

Cathleen *stops her wheel with a sudden movement, and leans out to listen.*

Nora We're to find out if it's Michael's they are, some time herself will be down looking by the sea.

Cathleen. How would they be Michael's, Nora? How would he go to the length of that way to the far north?

Nora. The young priest says he's known the like of it.

'If it's Michael's they are,' says he, 'you can tell herself he's got a clean burial, by the grace of God; and if they're not his, let no one say a word about them, for she'll be getting her death,' says he, 'with crying and lamenting.'

The door which Nora half closed is blown open by a gust of wind.

Cathleen *(looking out anxiously).* Did you ask him would he stop Bartley going this day with the horses to the Galway fair?

Nora. 'I won't stop him,' says he; 'but let you not be afraid. Herself does be saying prayers half through the night, and the Almighty God won't leave her destitute,' says he, 'with no son living.'

Cathleen. Is the sea bad by the white rocks, Nora?

Nora. Middling bad, God help us. There's a great roaring in the west, and it's worse it'll be getting when the tide's turned to the wind. *(She goes over to the table with the bundle).* Shall I open it now?

Cathleen. Maybe she'd wake up on us and come in before we'd done*(Coming to the table).* It's a long time we'll be, and the two of us crying.

Nora *(goes to the inner door and listens).* She's moving about on the bed. She'll be coming in a minute.

Cathleen. Give me the ladder, and I'll put them up in the turf-loft, the way she won't know of them at all, and maybe when the tide turns she'll be going down to see would he be floating from the east.

They put the ladder against the gable of the chimney.

Cathleen *goes up a few steps and hides the bundle in the turf-loft.* Maurya *comes from the inner room.*

Maurya *(looking up at* Cathleen *and speaking querulously).* Isn't it turf enough you have for this day and evening?

Cathleen. There's a cake baking at the fire for a short space *(throwing down the turf),* and Bartley will want it when the tide turns if he goes to Connemara.

Nora *picks up the turf and puts it round the pot-oven.*

Maurya *(sitting down on a stool at the fire).* He won't go this day with the wind rising from the south and west. He won't go this day, for the young priest will stop him surely.

Nora. He'll not stop him, mother; and I heard Eamon Simon and Stephen Pheety and Colum Shawn saying he would go.

Maurya. Where is he itself?

Nora. He went down to see would there be another boat sailing in the week, and I'm thinking it won't be long till he's here now, for the tide's turning at the green head, and the hooker's tacking from the east.

Cathleen. I hear some one passing the big stones.

Nora *(looking out).* He's coming now, and he in a hurry.

Bartley *(comes in and looks round the room. Speaking sadly and quietly).* Where is the bit of new rope, Cathleen, was bought in Connemara?

Cathleen *(coming down).* Give it to him, Nora; it's on a nail by the white boards. I hung it up this morning, for the pig with the black feet was eating it.

Nora *(giving him a rope).* Is that it, Bartley?

Maurya. You'd do right to leave that rope, Bartley, hanging by the boards. (Bartley *takes the rope*). It will be wanting in this place, I'm telling you, if Michael is washed up tomorrow morning or the next morning, or any morning in the week; for it's a deep grave we'll make him, by the grace of God.

Bartley *(beginning to work with the rope).* I've no halter the way I can ride down on the mare, and I must go now quickly. This is the one boat going for two weeks or beyond it, and the fair will be a good fair for horses, I heard them saying below.

Maurya. It's a hard thing they'll be saying below if the body is washed up and there's no man in it to make the coffin, and I after giving a big price for the finest white boards you'd find in Connemara.

She looks round at the boards.

Bartley. How would it be washed up, and we after looking each day for nine days, and a strong wind blowing a while back from the west and south?

Maurya. If it isn't found itself, that wind is raising the sea, and there was a star up against the moon, and it is rising in the night. If it was a hundred horses, or a thousand horses, you had itself, what is the price of a thousand horses against a son where there is one son only?

Bartley *(working at the halter, to* Cathleen). Let you go down each day, and see the sheep aren't jumping in on the rye, and if the jobber comes you can sell the pig with the black feet if there is a good price going.'

Maurya. How would the like of her get a good price for a pig?

Bartley *(to* Cathleen*).* If the west wind holds with the last bit of the moon let you and Nora get up weed enough for another cock for the kelp. It's hard set we'll be from this day with no one in it but one man to work.

Maurya. It's hard set we'll be surely the day you're drowned with the rest. What way will I live and the girls with me, and I an old woman looking for the grave?

Bartley *lays down the halter, takes off his old coat, and puts on a newer one of the same flannel.*

Bartley *(to* Nora*).* Is she coming to the pier?

Nora *(looking out)* She's passing the green head and letting fall her sails.

Bartley *(getting his purse and tobacco).* I'll have half an hour to go down, and you'll see me coming again in two days, or in three days, or maybe in four days if the wind is bad.

Maurya *(turning round to the fire, and putting her shawl over her head).* Isn't it a hard and cruel man won't hear a word from an old woman, and she holding him from the sea?

Cathleen. It's the life of a young man to be going on the sea, and who would listen to an old woman with one thing and she saying it over?

Bartley *(taking the halter).* I must go now quickly. I'll ride down on the red mare, and the grey pony'll run behind me.... The blessing of God on you.

He goes out.

Maurya *(crying out as he is in the door).* He's gone now, God spare us, and we'll not see him again. He's gone now, and when the black night is falling I'll have no son left me in the world.

Cathleen. Why wouldn't you give him your blessing and he looking round in the door? Isn't it sorrow enough is on every one in this house without you sending him out with an unlucky word behind him, and a hard word in his ear?

Maurya *takes up the tongs and begins raking the fire aimlessly without looking round.*

Nora *(turning towards her).* You're taking away the turf from the cake.

Cathleen *(crying out).* The Son of God forgive us, Nora, we're after forgetting his bit of bread. *(She comes over to the fire).*

Nora. And it's destroyed he'll be going till dark night, and he after eating nothing since the sun went up.

Cathleen *(turning the cake out of the oven).* It's destroyed he'll be, surely. There's no sense left on any person in a house where an old woman will be talking for ever.

Maurya *sways herself on her stool.*

Cathleen *(cutting off some of the bread and rolling it in a cloth; to* Maurya*).* Let you go down now to the spring well and give him this and he passing. You'll see him then and the dark word will be broken, and you can say 'God speed you,' the way he'll be easy in his mind.

Maurya *(taking the bread).* Will I be in it as soon as himself?

Cathleen. If you go now quickly.

Maurya *(standing up unsteadily).* It's hard set I am to walk.

Cathleen *(looking at her anxiously).* Give her the stick, Nora, or maybe she'll slip on the big stones.

Nora. What stick?

Cathleen. The stick Michael brought from Connemara.

Maurya *(taking a stick* Nora *gives her).* In the big world the old people do be leaving things after them for their sons and children, but in this place it is the young men do be leaving things behind for them that do be old.

She goes out slowly. Nora *goes over to the ladder.*

Cathleen. Wait, Nora, maybe she'd turn back quickly. She's that sorry, God help her, you wouldn't know the thing she'd do.

Nora. Is she gone round by the bush?

Cathleen *(looking out).* She's gone now. Throw it down quickly, for the Lord knows when she'll be out of it again.

Nora *(getting the bundle from the loft).* The young priest said he'd be passing tomorrow, and we might go down and speak to him below if it's Michael's they are surely.

Cathleen *(taking the bundle).* Did he say what way they were found?

Nora *(coming down).* 'There were two men,' says he, 'and they rowing round with poteen before the cocks crowed, and the oar of one of them caught the body, and they passing the black cliffs of the north.'

Cathleen *(trying to open the bundle).* Give me a knife, Nora; the string's perished with the salt water, and there's a black knot on it you wouldn't loosen in a week.

Nora *(giving her a knife).* I've heard tell it was a long way to Donegal.

Cathleen *(cutting the string).* It is surely. There was a man in here a while ago – the man sold us that knife – and he said if you set off walking from the rocks beyond, it would be in seven days you'd be in Donegal.

Nora. And what time would a man take, and he floating?

Cathleen *opens the bundle and takes out a bit of a shirt and a stocking. They look at them eagerly.*

Cathleen *(in a low voice).* The Lord spare us, Nora! isn't it a queer hard thing to say if it's his they are surely?

Nora. I'll get his shirt off the hook the way we can put the one flannel on the other. *(She looks through some clothes hanging* *in the corner).* It's not with them, Cathleen, and where will it be?

Cathleen. I'm thinking Bartley put it on him in the morning, for his own shirt was heavy with the salt in it. *(Pointing to the corner).* There's a bit of a sleeve was of the same stuff. Give me that and it will do.

Nora *brings it to her and they compare the flannel.*

Cathleen. It's the same stuff, Nora; but if it is itself, aren't there great rolls of it in the shops of Galway, and isn't it many another man may have a shirt of it as well as Michael himself?

Nora *(who has taken up the stocking and counted the stitches, crying out).* It's Michael, Cathleen, it's Michael; God spare his soul, and what will herself say when she hears this story, and Bartley on the sea?

Cathleen *(taking the stocking).* It's a plain stocking.

Nora. It's the second one of the third pair I knitted, and I put up three-score stitches, and I dropped four of them.

Cathleen *(counts the stitches).* It's that number is in it *(crying out).* Ah, Nora, isn't it a bitter thing to think of him floating that way to the far north, and no one to keen him but the black hags that do be flying on the sea?

Nora *(swinging herself half round, and throwing out her arms on the clothes).* And isn't it a pitiful thing when there is nothing left of a man who was a great rower and fisher but a bit of an old shirt and a plain stocking?

Cathleen *(after an instant).* Tell me is herself coming, Nora? I hear a little sound on the path.

Nora *(looking out).* She is, Cathleen. She's coming up to the door.

Cathleen. Put these things away before she'll come in. Maybe it's easier she'll be after giving her blessing to Bartley, and we won't let on we've heard anything the time he's on the sea.

Nora *(helping* Cathleen *to close the bundle).* We'll put them here in the corner.

They put them into a hole in the chimney corner. Cathleen *goes back to the spinning-wheel.*

Nora. Will she see it was crying I was?

Cathleen. Keep your back to the door the way the light'll not be on you.

Nora *sits down at the chimney corner, with her back to the door.* Maurya *comes in very slowly, without looking at the girls, and goes over to her stool at the other side of the fire. The cloth with the bread is still in her hand. The girls look at each other, and*

Nora *points to the bundle of bread.*

Cathleen *(after spinning for a moment).* You didn't give him his bit of bread?

Maurya *begins to keen softly, without turning round.*

Cathleen. Did you see him riding down?

Maurya *goes on keening.*

Cathleen *(a little impatiently).* God forgive you; isn't it a better thing to raise your voice and tell what you seen, than be making lamentation for a thing that's done? Did you see Bartley, I'm saying to you?

Maurya *(with a weak voice).* My heart's broken from this day.

Cathleen *(as before).* Did you see Bartley?

Maurya. I seen the fearfulest thing.

Cathleen *(leaves her wheel and looks out).* God forgive you; he's riding the mare now over the green head, and the grey pony behind him.

Maurya *(starts, so that her shawl falls back from her head and shows her white tossed hair. With a frightened voice).* The grey pony behind him...

Cathleen *(coming to the fire).* What is it ails you at all?

Maurya *(speaking very slowly).* I've seen the fearfulest thing any person has seen since the day Bride Dara seen the dead man with the child in his arms.

Cathleen *and* **Nora.** Uah.

They crouch down in front of the old woman at the fire.

Nora. Tell us what it is you seen.

Maurya. I went down to the spring well, and I stood there saying a prayer to myself. Then Bartley came along, and he riding on the red mare with the grey pony behind him *(she puts up her hands, as if to hide something from her eyes).* The Son of God spare us, Nora!

Cathleen. What is it you seen?

Maurya. I seen Michael himself.

Cathleen *(speaking softly).* You did not, mother. It wasn't Michael you seen, for his body is after being found in the far north, and he's got a clean burial, by the grace of God.

Maurya *(a little defiantly).* I'm after seeing him this day, and he riding and galloping. Bartley came first on the red mare, and I tried to say 'God speed you,' but something choked the words in my throat. He went by quickly; and 'the blessing of God on you,' says he, and I could say nothing. I looked up then, and I crying, at the grey pony, and there was Michael upon it – with fine clothes on him, and new shoes on his feet.

Cathleen *(begins to keen).* It's destroyed we are from this day. It's destroyed, surely.

Nora. Didn't the young priest say the Almighty God won't leave her destitute with no son living?

Maurya *(in a low voice, but clearly).* It's little the like of him knows of the sea... Bartley will be lost now, and let you call in Eamon and make me a good coffin out of the white boards, for I won't live after them. I've had a husband, and a husband's father, and six sons in this house – six fine men, though it was a hard birth I had with every one of them and they coming into the world – and some of them were found and some of them were not found, but they're gone now the lot of them... There was Stephen and Shawn were lost in the great wind, and found after in the Bay of Gregory of the Golden Mouth, and carried up the two of them on one plank, and in by that door.

She pauses for a moment, the girls start as if they heard something through the door that is half open behind them.

Nora *(in a whisper).* Did you hear that, Cathleen? Did you hear a noise in the north-east?

Cathleen *(in a whisper).* There's someone after crying out by the seashore.

Maurya *(continues without hearing anything).* There was Sheamus and his father, and his own father again, were lost in a dark night, and not a stick or sign was seen of them when the sun went up. There was Patch after was drowned out of a curagh that turned over. I was sitting here with Bartley, and he a baby lying on my two knees, and I seen two women, and three women, and four women coming in, and they crossing themselves and not saying a word. I looked out then, and there were men coming after them, and they holding a thing in the half of a red sail, and water dripping out of it – it was a dry day, Nora – and leaving a track to the door.

She pauses again with her hand stretched out towards the door. It opens softly and old women begin to come in, crossing themselves on the threshold, and kneeling down in front of the stage with red petticoats over their heads.

Maurya *(half in a dream, to* Cathleen*).* Is it Patch, or Michael, or what is it at all?

Cathleen. Michael is after being found in the far north, and when he is found there how could he be here in this place?

Maurya. There does be a power of young men floating round in the sea, and what way would they know if it was Michael they had, or another man like him, for when a man is nine days in the sea, and the wind blowing, it's hard set his own mother would be to say what man was in it.

Cathleen. It's Michael, God spare him, for they're after sending us a bit of his clothes from the far north.

She reaches out and hands Maurya *the clothes that belonged to Michael.* Maurya *stands up slowly, and takes them in her hands.* Nora *looks out.*

Nora. They're carrying a thing among them, and there's water dripping out of it and leaving a track by the big stones.

Cathleen *(in a whisper to the women who have come in).* Is it Bartley it is?

One of the Women. It is, surely, God rest his soul.

Two younger women come in and pull out the table. Then men carry in the body of Bartley, *laid on a plank, with a bit of a sail over it, and lay it on the table.*

Cathleen *(to the women as they are doing so).* What way was he drowned?

One of the Women. The grey pony knocked him over into the sea, and he was washed out where there is a great surf on the white rocks.

Maurya *has gone over and knelt down at the head of the table. The women are keening softly and swaying themselves with a slow movement.* Cathleen *and* Nora *kneel at the other end of the table. The men kneel near the door.*

Maurya *(raising her head and speaking as if she did not see the people around her).* They're all gone now, and there isn't anything more the sea can do to me... I'll have no call now to be up crying and praying when the wind breaks from the south and you can hear the surf is in the east, and the surf is in the west, making a great stir with the two noises, and they hitting one on the other. I'll have no call now to be going down and getting Holy Water in the dark nights after Samhain, and I won't care what way the sea is when the other women will be keening. (*To* Nora) Give me the Holy Water, Nora; there's a small sup still on the dresser.

Nora *gives it to her.*

Maurya *(drops Michael's clothes across* Bartley's *feet, and sprinkles the Holy Water over him).* It isn't that I haven't prayed for you, Bartley, to the Almighty God. It isn't that I haven't said prayers in the dark night till you wouldn't know what I'd be saying; but it's a great rest I'll have now, and it's time, surely. It's a great rest I'll have now, and great sleeping in the long nights after Samhain, if it's only a bit of wet flour we do have to eat, and maybe a fish that would be stinking.

She kneels down again, crossing herself, and saying prayers under her breath.

Cathleen *(to an old man).* Maybe yourself and Eamon would make a coffin when the sun rises. We have fine white boards herself bought. God help her, thinking Michael would be found, and I have a new cake you can eat while you'll be working.

The Old Man *(looking at the boards).* Are there nails with them?

Cathleen. There are not, Colum; we didn't think of the nails.

Another Man. It's a great wonder she wouldn't think of the nails, and all the coffins she's seen made already.

Cathleen. It's getting old she is, and broken.

Maurya *stands up again very slowly and spreads out the pieces of Michael's clothes beside the body, sprinkling them with the last of the Holy Water.*

Nora *(in a whisper to* Cathleen*).* She's quiet now and easy; but the day Michael was drowned you could hear her crying out from this to the spring well. It's fonder she was of Michael, and would anyone have thought that?

Cathleen *(slowly and clearly).* An old woman will be soon tired with anything she will do, and isn't it nine days herself is after crying and keening and making great sorrow in the house?

Maurya *(puts the empty cup mouth downwards on the table, and lays her hands together on Bartley's feet).* They're all together this time, and the end is come. May the Almighty God have mercy on Bartley's soul, and on Michael's soul, and on the souls of Sheamus and Patch, and Stephen and Shawn *(bending her head);* and may He have mercy on my soul, Nora, and on the soul of every one is left living in the world.

She pauses, and the keen rises a little more loudly from the women, then sinks away.

Maurya *(continuing).* Michael has a clean burial in the far north, by the grace of the Almighty God. Bartley will have a fine coffin out of the white boards, and a deep grave surely. What more can we want than that? No man at all can be living for ever, and we must be satisfied.

She kneels down again and the curtain falls slowly.

stories of the seanchaí

seán o'sullivan

All but one of these stories were originally published in Sean O'Sullivan's *Folktales of Ireland.* Sean O'Sullivan, born in Tuosist, Co. Kerry, is recognised as one of the foremost authorities on the Irish oral tradition. These stories, which he collected in various parts of the country, are typical examples of the art of the *Seanchaí,* handed down from generation to generation by word of mouth.

In former times each rural area had its own *Seanchaí* – an old man who combined a rich store of folklore with the ability to tell a story well. His neighbours would gather nightly to listen to the tales he related as he sat at the fireside.

The following were the qualities of a good *seanchaí:* he told stories often and he loved to tell them; he had an outstanding memory and was able to master a huge body of narratives and recite them perfectly; he had a musical voice both when speaking Gaelic and English; he used few bodily movements and spoke slowly; he knew when to pause for effect (especially after an important event in the story, to allow each listener to picture the event in his imagination and savour it), and these pauses were never more than ten seconds or so; he looked at each member of the audience, then down for a time, then into the fire for a time; and, he smiled but did not laugh after telling something amusing that aroused great merriment among his listeners.

The *seanchaí* never rose from the corner of the fireplace, and if he gestured too much in attempting to act out the story he was laughed at. No interruptions were allowed once the storytelling commenced. No one asked questions. No words of encouragement or praise were given as in singing and dancing. No one dared sleep, and no one wanted to when a good narrator held forth.

Here are a selection of stories told by a seanchaí:

A NARROW ESCAPE

IT WAS ON A FINE SUNDAY NIGHT many years ago, my father sent me to call the members of his crew as he had decided to moor some fishing nets in order to get bait to enable them to shoot the long lines for heavy ground fish on the following day. It being the Sabbath day he would not set the nets until after midnight. I was only a boy at the time but as one of the crew of four failed to turn up and the night was fine, my father allowed me to take his place in the four-man curagh.

It was a bright starlit night and when the nets were moored about a mile from the shore we started to row homewards when we saw the lights of a ship coming from the open sea through the Sound. As my father was a ship's pilot we immediately raced for the approaching ship. After about half an hour's hard pulling the lights appeared to be as far away as when we first saw them, so we eased up to watch them for a few minutes. My father took his match box out and cracked several matches to attract the attention of those on board, and as if in answer to those signals the ship seemed to swing round towards us and was aglow with lights that we had not seen before. "He has seen our lights now," said one of the men and we continued to row harder than ever towards him, but although we went a considerable distance this time, it seemed to us that he was as far away as ever.

We were now several miles from our own shore and drawing closer to the towering Cliffs of Moher where there was no landing place for miles on either side, a most dangerous coast indeed and more so at night. Suddenly we noticed that it had grown darker; the sky had become overcast and a rough swell in the sea had set in. The ship's lights had grown dim and finally disappeared entirely. There was nothing to do now but to make for home so the curagh was turned about.

We had not pulled half a dozen strokes when, there off our stern, within two cables-length, lay a big ship ablaze with lights. We were all excited now and about went the curagh again as we made for the ship with all speed, but although we rowed hard for fully fifteen minutes, she appeared as far away as before.

I had noticed for some time now that my father was paying little attention to the ship but was looking at the sky and at the sea. He had been silent for some time, but now he ordered us to pull for home with all speed. The ship's lights had grown very dim again, so we headed for home. I was very disappointed as I had expected to be able to go aboard a big ship for the first time and see the foreign sailors and get some ship's biscuits and maybe a coconut and some nice souvenirs from the ship's officers.

The sea had by now got rather rough, with strong gusts of wind. After a long hard pull we got back close to the strand from where we had put off, and by that time we had almost forgotten about the ship as it required all our skill and vigilance in the darkness to avoid the short, steep lumps of sea and prevent any of them coming aboard and swamping us. As it was, we were shipping a lot of water and I was kept bailing it out as fast as it came in. Once as we rode on the crest of a wave one of the men cried out that he saw the ship lights again, but my father silenced him by saying that the sooner we could get ashore the better.

When we had got within a few hundred yards of the beach there was a lull; the wind died away and it became quite calm. One of the men remarked that it was going to be a good night after all, but my father said that there would be a sudden shift of wind at any moment and it would be worse presently. We hauled up the curragh, got it into its place and had just secured it when the shift of wind came. It came with a roar and blew right in on the beach, lashing the sea into a fury and almost taking us off our own feet.

Had we been a few minutes later in getting ashore it would have caught us. Our curragh could never have weathered the heavy seas, and we should have been swamped in trying to run for the beach. "We were very lucky to be ashore before it came," said one of the men, "we were just in time." "It was all because of that queer ship," said another. They then separated and went home.

Before going to bed I was tempted to have another look to see if the ship was in sight, and there, close in off the strand, much nearer than where our nets were moored, was a vessel with many-coloured lights. I ran and excitedly told my father, who was kneeling down beside the fire saying his rosary before going to bed. He motioned me to be silent and shut the door, after which I went to bed, and falling asleep, dreamt about ships and sailors, coconuts and ship's biscuits, panama straw hats and leather waist-bands with beautiful designs.

I awoke about daybreak and looked out. The storm had spent itself but there was still a strong breeze blowing in on the strand. After starting the fire and putting on the kettle, I went to see if any wreckage had been washed ashore. I picked up an empty tin which had contained some ship's biscuits, and further on I found a coconut cracked in two and, of course, empty.

THE CHILDREN OF THE DEAD WOMAN

THERE WAS A MAN LONG AGO, and he was looking for a wife. He found one, but he was only a year married to her when she died, while giving birth to a child. Her mother was anxious to have the child to rear, but the father said that he would not give the child away to anybody. He would try to rear it himself. At that time, there were old women who earned their living by minding children; so the father got one of them to look after his own child. The only people in the house besides the child were this old woman and himself. He was a very strong man. Two months went by. The old woman slept in a bed beside the fire with the cradle nearby, so that she was able to attend to the child by night and by day.

One stormy evening, the father came home from his work. He took off his boots and sat beside the fire.

He took up the child, saying, "You are doing well, my little orphan, and getting strong."

"May God give you long life," said he to the old woman. "You are minding him well, to say that he is thriving so fast!"

"You don't know what I know," replied the old woman. "Every night since she died – at least, since I came here – that child's mother comes here. She eats some boiled potatoes and drinks some milk from the cupboard. The moment she comes in, she goes over to the cradle and kisses the child. Then she warms her hands at the fire before taking the boiled potatoes and milk from the cupboard. When she has taken some food, she comes to the cradle again, takes up the child, and feeds him at her breast. Then she washes him, puts dry clothes under him and lays him down in the cradle, kissing him. She then stands in the middle of the floor, looks up toward the room, where you are asleep, heaves a sigh, and goes out the door. She has done that every night since I came here. I see her, but I don't ask her any question."

"Had I known that," said the man, "and had I seen her, I would have held her here or failed in the attempt."

"You'll get your chance," said the old woman. "I will cough tonight when she comes. Have your ears open."

That night he did not take off all of his clothes but lay on the bed, so that he would see her when she came and hold her.

Late that night, they heard the door opening. She came in and kissed the child; then she went to the cupboard, got the dish of potatoes and the naggin of milk – naggins were common vessels at that time – and ate quickly. She then stirred up the fire and warmed herself. (I'd say she was cold). When she had warmed herself, she went to the cradle, took up the child, suckled him, washed and cleaned him, and put dry clothes under him. Then she stood in the middle of the floor and looked up toward the room. The old woman coughed, and the woman went out the door.

"Are you awake now?" asked the old woman.

"I am," replied the man, coming down from the room.

"Did you see her?"

"I did, but I was too frightened to go near her. And I thought that if I saw her at all, I'd hold her here."

The two of them did not go to bed until it dawned. The man went next morning to the house of his wife's parents. Her three brothers were there, two of them were strong, hefty fellows, but the third was a weakling. The family welcomed him and asked him how the child was doing. He told them the child was thriving, that his mother came each night to wash and clean and suckle him.

"I saw her myself last night," said he. "She ate some potatoes and drank milk after attending to the child. Then she went out the door, and I was too frightened to move."

"Bad luck to you," said the eldest brother. "If you saw her, you could have held her. If I were there, I'd not let her go."

"Well, come over to me tonight then, and you'll see her," said the husband. "We'll see if you can hold her."

"If I see her, I'll hold her," said the brother.

They walked back to the house again. The old woman and the child were there. When they sat down, the dead woman's brother asked the old woman did his sister come every night. She said that she did.

"Well, if I see her tonight, I won't let her go," said he.

Early in the night, the dead woman's husband and brother went up to the bedroom and kept watch to see if she would come. It wasn't long until they heard the door opening. Her brother saw her as well as the husband and the old woman. She went up to the fire and warmed her hands. (I suppose she was always cold). When she had warmed herself, she went to the cupboard, took out the dish of potatoes and a naggin of milk and ate quickly. Then she went to the cradle, took up the child, and put him to her breast. She cleaned and washed him and put dry clothes under him. Then she stood in the middle of the floor, looked up toward the room, heaved a sigh, and went out.

"Are ye asleep?" asked the old woman.

"No," they replied, as they came down from the room.

"Ye are the two most cowardly men I've ever met," said the old woman.

(I must shorten my story for you now). The same thing happened to the second brother.

"May the devil take ye!" said the third brother. "If I were there, I'd hold her."

"Bad cess to you! You're able to do nothing," replied the two brothers.

"I'll tell ye what I can do," said the youngest brother. "If I saw my sister, I'd hold her and wouldn't let her go. If ye come along with me tonight, ye'll see that I'll hold her if I lay eyes on her."

The three brothers went to the house that night. Before it was too late, they decided to go up to the bedroom. They lay down, the youngest on the outside, so that he could easily run down to the kitchen to catch his sister. It wasn't long until they heard the door opening, and in she came. They all saw her. She ran to the fire and warmed her hands. Then she went to the cupboard and took out the potatoes and milk. She seemed to be very hungry. After eating, she sat down and took the child from the cradle and put him to her breast; then she washed and cleaned him and put dry clothes under and about him.

As she put him back into the cradle, she kissed him three times. On the other nights, she had kissed him only once. She then stood up to leave. Weren't the four men great cowards that they made no move? Just then, up jumped the youngest brother, and he put his two arms around her. She screamed and begged him, for God's sake, to let her go. In the struggle, she lifted him up to the rafters, beseeching him to release her.

"I'll be killed if I'm not back in time," she cried.

"The devil a foot will you put out of here," said her brother.

She was dragging him about, almost killing him; so he shouted to one of his brothers to come to his assistance. The pair of them struggled with her until she finally fell down on the floor in a dead faint. The youngest brother still kept his hold of her.

Next morning, her husband went with one of the brothers for the priest. When they came back, the priest prayed over her until ten o'clock, while her young brother held her. When she recovered her speech, she told the priest that that was to have been her last visit, as the fairies with whom she stayed were moving to Ulster that night. So she stayed with her husband and child, much the same as she had been before, except that she had a wild look in her eyes till the day she died. She bore nine sons to her husband after her rescue, and they came to be known as the children of the dead woman.

THE COW THAT ATE THE PIPER

THERE WERE THREE SPALPEENS coming home to Kerry from Limerick one time after working there. On their way, they met a piper on the road.

"I'll go along with ye," said the piper.

"All right," they said.

The night was very cold, freezing hard, and they were going to perish. They saw a dead man on the road with a new pair of shoes on his feet.

"By heavens!" said the piper, "I haven't a stitch of shoes on me. Give me that spade to see can I cut off his legs."

"Twas the only way he could take off the shoes. They were held on by the frost. So he took hold of the spade and cut off the two feet at the ankles. He took them along with him. They got lodgings at a house where three cows were tied in the kitchen.

"Keep away from that gray cow," said the servant girl, "or she'll eat your coats. Keep out from her."

They all went to sleep. The three spalpeens and the piper stretched down near the fire. The piper heated the shoes and the dead man's feet at the fire and got the shoes off. He put on the shoes and threw the feet near the gray cow's head. Early next morning, he left the house wearing his new pair of shoes. When the servant girl got up, she looked at the door. It was bolted, and the three spalpeens were asleep near the fire.

"My God!" she cried. "There were four of ye last night, and now there are only three. Where did the other man go?"

"We don't know," they said. "How would we know where he went?"

She went to the gray cow's head and found the two feet.

"Oh my!" she cried. "He was eaten by her."

She called the man of the house.

"The gray cow has eaten one of the men," said she.

"What's that you're saying?" said the farmer.

"I'm telling the truth," said she. "There's only his feet left. The rest of him is eaten."

The farmer got up. "There were four of ye there last night, men," said he.

"There were," said one of the spalpeens, "and our comrade has been eaten by the cow."

"Don't cause any trouble about it," said the farmer. "Here's five pounds for ye. Eat your breakfast and be off. Don't say a word."

They left when they had the breakfast eaten. And they met the piper some distance from the house, and he dancing on the road. Such a thing could happen!

THE MARCH COCK AND THE COFFIN

THERE WAS A HOUSE IN THIS TOWNLAND, in which I am telling my story, and a man lived there with his wife and children. The man worked every day not far from the house, and whenever he looked toward the house, he would see a coffin descending from the sky on the side of the house. At the same moment each day, the March cock, which was in the house, used to jump up, shake his wings, and crow loudly. Then he used to try to fly up on the gable, and if he couldn't do that, he would settle on the chimney and keep crowing until he banished the coffin.

That went on for three weeks or so, and the man saw it happening each day. The woman of the house came to hate the cock on account of its crowing. Then one day, when the man was in the field, he saw the coffin coming down on the side of the house. The cock was inside in the house and he jumped up, shook his wings, and started to crow. The woman was so annoyed that she took up a wooden mallet and threw it at the cock to drive him from the house, so that she wouldn't be listening to him. She hit the cock on the head and killed him with the blow. The coffin remained where it was. The man was worried and he went to the house and found the cock dead.

"Who killed the cock?" he asked.

"I did," said his wife. "My head was split from his crowing day after day. I threw the mallet at him to drive him away, but I struck him on the head and killed him."

"My seven thousand curses on you!" said the husband. "You killed the cock and you killed me too!"

He lay down on the bed, and in three days' time, he was dead.

That's as true a story as was ever told. It happened here in this townland, and the house where the man and the cock were can still be seen by anybody.

The dear blessing of God and of the Church on the souls of the dead! And may we be seventeen hundred thousand times better off a year from tonight – ourselves and all who are listening to me.

THE UGLIER FOOT

THERE WAS A TAILOR IN BALLYVOURNEY a long time ago. He had very big ankles, and the nickname the people had on him was Tadhg of the Ankles. At that time, tradesmen travelled from house to house, and the people used to gather up for sport and fun with them.

One night Tadhg was sewing away, sitting on the table, and he had one of his legs stretched out from him. The woman of the house was sitting at the head of the table, between Tadhg and the fire. She noticed Tadhg's big ankle.

"Upon my conscience, that's an ugly foot," said she. One or two people laughed at this.

"Upon my conscience," said Tadhg, "there's a still uglier foot than it in the house."

The woman of the house must have had badly shaped feet herself, and she thought that Tadhg was hinting at her.

"There isn't an uglier foot than it in the whole world," said she.

"Would you lay a bet on that?" asked Tadhg.

"I would," said she.

"I'll bet you a quart of whiskey that there's an uglier foot than it in this house," said Tadhg.

"I'll take the bet," said the woman.

At that, Tadhg pulled his other foot from under him.

"Now," said he, "which is the uglier, the first foot or the second one?"

"Upon my word, the second is a lot uglier," said the woman.

"Very well," said Tadhg. "Send out for a quart of whiskey for me."

"I will, indeed," said the woman.

She was glad to have lost the bet when her own feet weren't compared to Tadhg's.

THE FOX AND THE EAGLE

THERE CAME A VERY BAD YEAR one time. One day the fox was near the shore of the Lakes of Killarney, and he couldn't find a bird or anything else to eat. Then he spied three ducks a bit out from the shore and thought to himself that if he could catch hold of them, he would have a fine meal. There was some water parsnip with very large leaves growing by the shore, and he swam out to it and cut off two big leaves of it with his teeth. He held one of them at each side of his mouth and swam towards the ducks. They never felt anything until he had taken one of them off with him.

Very satisfied with himself, he brought her ashore, laid her down, and decided to try and catch the other two as well – 'tis seldom they would be on offer!

He caught a second duck by the same trick and left her dead near the first. Then out he swam for the third and brought her in. But, if he did, there was no trace of the other two where he had left them.

"May God help me!" said he. "I have only the one by my day's work. What'll I do? I wonder who is playing tricks on me."

He looked all around but couldn't see an enemy anywhere. Then he looked towards the cliff that was nearby, and what did he spy but the nest of an eagle high up on it.

"No one ever took my two ducks but the eagle," said he. "As good as I am at thieving, there's a bigger thief above my head."

He didn't know how to get at the eagle. Then he saw a fire smouldering not far away, where men had been working at a quarry a few days before. They had a fire and it was still burning slowly under the surface of the ground. He dragged the duck to the fire and pulled her hither and thither through the embers. Then he left her down on the grass and hid. The eagle must have been watching out for the third duck too, for down he swooped and snatched her up to his nest. No sooner did the dead duck's body touch the dry nest than the nest caught fire – there were live embers stuck in the duck's feathers. Down fell the blazing nest with the three dead ducks as well as the eagle's three young ones inside it, so the fox had six birds for his supper. Didn't he get his own back well on the eagle?

ACKNOWLEDGEMENTS

We would like to thank Ann Jackson and Brian Kavanagh for work in the development of the materials; Tim O'Neill for reading and commenting on the manuscript; Mr. Seamus Heaney for 'The Evening Land', 'Inisheer' and 'The Oarsman's Song'; A. D. Peters and Co. Ltd. for extracts from *Famine* by Liam O'Flaherty; for extracts from *The Islanders* by Tomas O'Crohan, by permission of the Oxford University Press; Dr. Brendan Kennelly for 'Sea'; for 'Years Later' from 'The Cleggan Disaster' reprinted by permission of Faber and Faber Ltd. from *Sailing to an Island* by Richard Murphy; for 'The Thatcher' reprinted by permission of Faber and Faber Ltd. from *Door into the Dark* by Seamus Heaney; Wolfhound Press for 'The Test of Courage' from *The Pedlar's Revenge and Other Stories* (1976) by Liam O'Flaherty; Jonathan Cape Ltd., for 'Spring Sowing', 'The Letter' and 'Going into Exile' from *The Short Stories of Liam O'Flaherty;* Mrs. Kate Mulkerrins and Chatto and Windus for 'A Day's Hunting' from Maurice O'Sullivan's *Twenty Years A-Growing;* the University of Chicago Press and Sean O'Sullivan for 'The Children of the Dead Woman', 'The Cow that ate the Piper', 'The March Cock and the Coffin', 'The Uglier Foot' and 'The Fox and the Eagle' from *Folk Tales of Ireland.*

In instances where we have failed to trace the copyright holder, we would be grateful if they would contact the publisher.

We would like to thank the following for permission to reproduce photographs: Pat Langan and *The Irish Times* pages 2 and 3, 6, 10, 18 bottom, 23, 24, 34, 48, 61, 65, 76, 80, 95, 98 bottom, 100, 113, 117, 119, 121, 133, 137, 149, 153, 159, 161, 168, 172, 179, 190, 197, 214, 226, 237. Bord Failte Eireann pages 18 top, 27, 30, 41 top, 20, 47, 67, 70, 85, 87, 93, 98 top, 129 bottom, 157, 162, 184; The Director of the National Museum of Ireland pages 24, 37, 41 bottom, 42, 52, 55, 60, 129 top, The Director of the National Library of Ireland pages 106, 107, 111, 141, 145, 203.